DISCLAIMER

THE HUNTERS is a work of fiction. The novel is written in the vernacular of the time, but no offense is intended to persons of any race, color or creed.

Dave Lloyd

BOOKS and SHORT STORIES
by DAVE LLOYD

FICTION
The Pistol
Outlaw

The Montana Saga
The Rebels - book one
Pardners - book two
T.S. Grounds - book three
Home Ranch - book four

Riverboat Trilogy
Fort Sarpy - book one
Upriver - book two
Captains - book three

Books of Short Stories
Tales
Arikara and Lord Guest

Ben Hite (Sharpshooter) Trilogy
Sharpshooter – book one
The Hunters – book two
Legacy – book three

NON-FICTION

History of Early Rosebud

DEDICATION

Life, Liberty & the Pursuit
of Good Books

THE HUNTERS
SEQUEL to SHARPSHOOTER

by

DAVE LLOYD

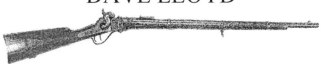

PART I

CHAPTER 1.

Ben Hite dipped his hands in the wash bowl's hot water and once again reflected that a rancher's usual work day left him much cleaner than he'd been when he'd worked as a freighter, fighting constant dust or mud on the trail. He was also usually warmer than he'd been working as a miner, wading in ice cold water. He turned and grabbed a dry, clean towel from the rack and scrubbed his face and hands dry, then handed it to Freddy, who was standing waiting for it, having just washed his own face and hands before they sat down to eat supper. Ben noticed that the boy was growing a little facial fuzz and was about to tease him, then thought better of it. Freddy was pretty thin-skinned and might take it wrong.

They went into the big dining room and to their places at the long table, groaning with a rich bounty of dishes filled with meat, potatoes, beans, bread, gravy and side dishes of butter and jelly, courtesy of the wild plums and chokecherry bushes which had lately ripened and provided Moira, Siccoolum and the girls with the means to put up jars and jars of jelly, syrup and jerked meat Siccoolum called pemmican, which had been dried and mixed with the berries, topped with tallow, then placed in the big root cellar they had dug that summer.

Its shelves had been loaded with the provisions they had put up for winter: preserved meats, primarily buffalo and elk, though there were birds and fish, also, berries of several kinds, including raspberries from the patch that Siccoolum had found and transplanted, vegetables from the Metis' gardens they had traded for, and their own patch, and some canned goods that Ben had bought in Benton and freighted out to the ranch. Now, the root cellar was filled with food to overflowing and the winter's food supply was assured, though Ben wanted to do some hunting and hang a couple buffalo cows and an elk or two before snow flew.

The wood supply had been cut, hauled down from the foothills and stacked in several piles about the places. After the debacle of the stable fire down in Salt Lake, Ben was careful to separate stables, hay stacks and wood piles and other flammable items into smaller entities so that losing one didn't mean that they would lose them all. The bunkhouse had its own wood pile, as did the big house, and Moira and Miles's house. The barn and the two stables had their own hay stacks and lofts. The root cellar at the big house was one of three: one at Moira's, and a small one out away from the place, by the creek. This one held some bare necessities in case they might need them in some emergency and it was well hidden from casual view.

Ben was satisfied that his family was well ready for another hard winter. They had a good amount of hay up this year, with the help of the Metis, and the horses should be able to survive the cold months pretty well. The spring fed creek iced over in places but it was easy for the animals to paw down to water, usually. If it did freeze too hard, someone would go down to cut a hole for them with an axe. With sufficient water, feed, and shelter from the wind, the horses and cows would fare well. He didn't want a repeat of the last winter, with all of them working hard to keep enough willows cut to feed to the horses to get them through.

Seated at the head, Ben listened with a grin as the table resounded with laughter, teasing and the talking of seven children, five women and seven men, all of whom seemed in high spirits as the summer's work came to a close. He tapped on his glass and said,

"Well, folks, let's ask Miles for the blessing."

He wasn't a particularly religious man but liked to observe the amenities, and with the children present, it seemed important to him and the others, he knew, to show a good example. Miles obliged and with the 'Amens' sounding, Ben started the big meat platter, filled to overflowing with elk steak tonight, around to his left, after spearing a couple large pieces for his own plate.

The group dug in, even Felice, Ketchum's girl friend from the Metis community, who had been shy around them. Bless had wasted no time in ferreting out another woman, a small, dark, flashing eyed vixen who seemed to be infatuated with the crippled freighter. Ben hoped so. Louie had told him that she was a widow with no children. A hard worker and a decent woman, he'd said. And Ketchum seemed to be captivated, so that was good. He needed to forget the Mormon woman he'd left behind in Salt Lake. She had betrayed them, anyway, to the Militia. Bad luck to her.

Between Siccoolum and Moira, on that side of the table, were the two high chairs for Moira's kids, Ben Junior, the baby and the little girl, Daisy, then the Mormon girl, Abigail, who was waving her spoon and laughing at something Kittledge had said, Brig, the boy, who was smiling, also, then Tommy Owens, who was growing fast and seemed to have a bottomless pit when it came to food. He was occupied with his plate, which was overflowing, but would soon be empty, Ben knew, and ready for seconds, which would not be withheld. Ben liked to see the youngsters eat and consequently, much food was cooked each and every day. The only one of his brood who wasn't an eater, was Betty, who seemed to have trouble keeping her food down lately.

He wondered what her problem was. She didn't look sick and had always before been almost as good at

3

putting food away as her brother, Freddy, who probably had the largest appetite of all of them. He'd have to ask Moira. She might know what ailed her sister.

* * *

Out on the porch later, Ben indulged himself in a pipe of the mellow new tobacco that Lakey had dropped off the last time through. It was a Virginia blend and had an aromatic smell to it that the kids all liked. He blew smoke rings for little Abigail, who liked to poke her fingers through them and make the babies laugh. Ben was crawling a little and Daisy was walking, both sturdy little kids who liked to come to Ben's knees and demand to be taken up to sit with him as he relaxed in the big chair he'd made from willows and buffalo robes. Kittledge would take out his mouth harp and the music would begin, with Miles tuning his fiddle, Ketchum his banjo and Moira trying to keep up with her pianoforte, which Ben had ordered for her not long ago, thinking she would like it at her house.

But with the porch at the big house being where everyone congregated, and Katy wanting to learn to play also, she had asked him if she might leave it just inside the door, so she could join in with the rest. Siccoolum had given her ready consent, as she liked the jam sessions as well as any, though she didn't play an instrument, just joined them at times with some gourd rattles she had made herself. Ben didn't either, though if the others had really gotten inquisitive, he might have owned up to having messed with a jew's harp when he was younger, during the war.

As it was, he just liked to listen and occasionally accompany the sing-alongs, if he knew the songs. It was all enjoyable and he liked the evenings they got together. It happened at least once, sometimes twice a week.

4

Later that night, he was about to head for bed, when he decided to go out to the outhouse and get rid of some supper. He went out the back door to the little building and was sitting there in the dark, when he heard a distant shot, then, as he listened, another. It sounded like it was over at Moira and Miles' place. They had taken their babies and gone for home when it was getting dark and just before that, Ketchum and his sweetheart had announced that they were riding back to her abode, the Metis' community on Cottonwood Creek.

Now, as Ben finished his business, he heard another sound, a dog barking. It was Willie, one of Brutus's pups whom Moira had taken a liking to and adopted for her own. Alarmed, Ben ran from the outhouse to the dark big house, to meet Siccoolum at the back door, already up and with his weapons in hand.

"Sounds like trouble over at Moira's! Stay here but fort up, lock and bar the doors. Get Freddy up and have him go wake Kittledge. The two of you stay here 'til I get back."

He made sure his Colt was loaded, as was his Henry, then took off at a run in the dark, sure of the familiar trail to the other house. Indian raids were infrequent now, but still a menace, with stock usually the target of the war parties, not white scalps. He was worried, though, about the shots. They'd been light repeater shots, likely a Henry or the new Winchesters.

He heard the thudding of distant horses going away as he came over the slight hill, his night vision operating well but seeing nothing off toward the sound. The house was dimly lit with a lantern in the kitchen and he stepped up on the porch, calling out softly,

"Moira . . . Honey, It's me, Ben."

The front door was partially open and now a baby began crying, little Ben Jr. He stopped and listened for an instant, then he pushed the door to and saw her lying by the table, blood running from her head. The baby was in its bassinet, sitting there by her side. Daisy was nowhere to be seen. He stepped to her and turning her over, saw she'd been tomahawked and partially scalped, her head caved where the blow had taken her on the right temple and forehead. She was still alive and came to for an instant as he moved her, her hand coming up and clutching his. She pressed it and whispered something, then was still. Ben knew she was gone and hugged her to him, tears running down his face as he rocked her in his arms.

Time passed and he felt a damp muzzle pushing against his face—-young Willie, the half-grown pup. He laid her gently back down, wiped his face and took stock, the rage building in his chest so that he could hardly breathe, the pounding of his heart pulsing in his eyes. The baby was crying and that sound, as much as Willie, woke him to his situation. He blew out the lamp, then, and working to regain his night vision, stepped to the door and listened. The night was quiet and presently he went through the portal and down to the yard, where he paused to listen again, then, his vision acute, went down to the corrals.

Half-way there, he nearly stumbled on Miles, his arms flung out in front of him. He was dead and scalped, but looked like he might have put up a fight before being killed. Probably that was his shooting that Ben had heard, though his gun was gone. Ben remembered that he had been carrying it when he'd left for home. The corrals were empty, which didn't surprise Ben. The raiders were after horses, but had no qualms about taking a white scalp or two along with them. Miles had likely heard them as they were getting the horses from the corrals. Willie might have alerted him. Likely they'd left a sentry back and he'd followed Miles, then killed him and gone back to the house to get Moira's scalp. But why would they have taken little Daisy?

6

* * *

Walking back, the baby in his arms still softly crying, he thought of its mother, lying dead in the house of which she had been so proud. She'd been a good mother, a hard worker, and a wife Miles had cherished, he knew. His daughter. Rage rode him hard as he entered his yard and yelled,

"It's me! Comin' in!"

The door opened to the dark house and Freddy stood there, his rifle in his hands, Kittledge beside him. Siccoolum was in the shadow, her carbine at the ready, also. He handed her the baby and said, "They're both dead—-scalped. And Daisy's gone. They took the horses and her, looks like. Unless they killed her out somewheres. Hev to wait 'til it gits light to see for sure, I guess." Betty and Katy, hearing what he'd just said, both let out screams as they realized their sister was dead.

He passed a hand over his face. "I'm goin' after 'em. Kitt, It's up to you and Bless to hold the place. An' someone'll have to take keer of the bodies. "

The group standing there in the kitchen saw Ben's face in the lantern light and were silent. Siccoolum handed the baby off to the crying girls and went out the door, grabbing up her carbine. As she headed for the barn, Ben caught up to her and said, "Listen, Luv, I'll be goin' fast. I don't think you should come."

She turned on him and snarled, her face a mask of pure ferocity. "I go! She was my sister! I go!"

He stepped back a little at her outburst, then gave up to the inevitable. If he left her, she'd just follow, as she had before. Better to have her up where he could watch her. Together, they went on down to the corral, to find it empty. Somehow the raiders had gathered the horses there, too, and made off with them without anyone at the house hearing them go, even Brutus and his mate, a big

7

yellow cur hound they called Cheater. Now, they were stymied until they could find mounts. Ben, cussing a blue streak, decided to walk to the trading post and see what they might have kept, if anything. He assured Siccoolum he would come back for her when he'd rounded up some horses and she went to help Kittledge with the bodies.

* * *

The sun was just coming up when he made it to the post, to find a beehive of activity. There was a large party of Indians there. Crow, it soon was apparent, who had followed the raiders from their village on the Bighorn, which had also been hit. The post too, had been cleaned of horses, even to their race mare and the stud which had been tied right up by the buildings. Major Reed brought a tall Crow warrior up to Ben as he stood there, after telling the two traders of what had transpired back at his place.

"This here's Many Coups, a damn good Injun, who's bin on their trail from his camp. He sez they's Blackfeet—-Piegan from up north. A big war party. He sez there's about twenty of 'em. They'll be headin' for the Missouri. The Crow'll try to catch up with 'em and get our horses back. Mebbe! Blackfeet're slick. Likely, they'll come up to another war party of theirs who'll cover their retreat fer 'em while the ones with the herd run past and make their getaway. 'Fraid we're back to Shank's mare fer awhile, damn it." He waved a casual hand toward each of them by way of introductions. "This here's Ben Hite."

While Reed had been talking, Ben had been studying the features of the brave standing before him. He liked what he saw. An Indian no longer young, but still lean and strong, with an open countenance and wide set eagle eyes that looked straight at those he faced. He carried a big Winchester '76 that had seen hard use but still was well cared for. A shell belt full of .50/95 cartridges was slung over his shoulder and a belt around his middle carried a beaded scabbard with a long bowie knife on his right, a steel-headed tomahawk on his left. His legs were encased in leather fringed leggins, and his feet in moccasins. His still black hair was braided with a single eagle feather protruding from it at the back of his head. He and Ben studied one another and then the Indian stuck out his hand and Ben gripped it in his own.

He said something and Ben turned to Reed, who translated. "Says he's heard of you. Seems the Bannacks bin talkin' 'bout ye. Sez ye killed some bad white men over in the Passamoiri valley an' ye got a Gros Ventre squaw who's killed a couple men herself. He wants to know if yer comin' along with 'em." Reed laughed wryly. "Not unless ye walk, I guess."

Ben was looking over his shoulder down the creek. "Tell him "Yes." He nodded at the brave, then said, pointing, "Here comes Siccoolum with a couple horses. Looks like Snake pulled his usual stunt on some Blackfeet. And Siccoolum must have had her black staked out away from the rest of the herd."

The others turned and looked at the sight of the Indian woman astride a sleek black horse, her own, and leading the saddled sorrel, jug-headed Snake which the traders had previously owned. Reed shook his head.

"That damn horse is a caution. Look! He still hez the catch rope on his jaw some Blackfoot got on 'im. Bet he caught him up, crawled aboard and ole' Snake threw 'im sky high. Couldn't ride him 'er even git his rope off 'im, is my guess."

Sure enough, the horse still did have a catch rope on his jaw, which was the way Indians rode their horses. Siccoolum came up and threw the rope to Ben, who caught it. She looked at the Crow crowded around and grunted something. Ben knew her tribe, the Gros Ventre, and the Crow were usually enemies, so he could guess that whatever she said was uncomplimentary. The Crow whooped. Many Coups said something to Reed, grinning.

9

He said, "She called the Crow "Louse Eaters!" He laughed. "She's quite a gal! Sure ya don't want to sell her?"

"Not interested. Got some candy in thet store?"

Reed was mystified, but nodded. "Need some travelin' food? Sure, I'll git'cha a sack of it."

He went in and shoveled a small sack full of hard candy and came back out, handing it to Ben, who said,

"Much obliged, put it on my bill. And some more ammo fer my Henry and the Colt. We'll settle up when I git back."

Bowles said, spitting a gob of tobacco, "If'n ye git back." He smiled a brown toothed grin. "Probably be plantin' yerself right'chere. That there horse'll throw you higher'n a tree an'stob yer head in the ground, I'd bet."

Ben took a piece of candy from the sack and gave it to Snake, who nibbled it up out of his hand, then watched quietly as Ben swung aboard. Reed exclaimed,

"Shit sakes! So that was ole Hang-Feather's trick! Always wondered how that ole Injun ever got that horse rode. How'd you find out he had to be bribed?"

"Used yer rot-gut whiskey an' bribed the Injun. He tole me the horse wanted to be asked afore he let someone on his back. Hard candy does the job well as anythin'. His favorite, though, is fried bread."

The Crow mounted and rode out, with Ben and Siccoolum following. Ben saw that the traders were content to stay behind.

CHAPTER 2.

The Crow rode fast on the trail of the herd. Ben counting, saw that there were thirty warriors, some pulling pack horses along loaded with their war gear. All were well armed, with repeaters or single shot breechloaders, usually carbines like Siccoolum's, which were easier to handle aboard a horse.

He'd tried to get her to change to a repeater, but she liked her Sharps and kept it oiled and handy, even in the kitchen as she cooked. She packed the new Colt pistol he'd given her, though, and could shoot it well. Like his, it was a .45 Single action Army revolver, but a cut-down version called a Sheriff's Model, bone handled, with a three inch barrel, and she packed it in a special pocket she'd made in her elk-skin skirt. In a separate pocket, she carried shells for the pistol. Around her middle was a large man's cartridge belt, cut down, with rifle shells, and from which hung two knives, one large, one small, which she used according to the job at hand. She rode astride in her split skirt, in an Indian saddle of her own making, with small stirrups from which the toes of her moccasins just protruded.

She made a fetching but martial sight and it generated some bantering talk among the Crow as they rode. She ignored it, though Ben had the idea that she could likely understand at least some of what was said. He was proud of her.

Ben rode his own saddle, which Siccoolum had thrown on Snake after catching him up. She said he was down at the creek watering when she was getting back after finding her black still where she'd picketed him the night before. Evidently, the Blackfeet had caught the sorrel all right, but failed to get him rode, so left him back rather than alert the house. She had brought Ben's Sharps in its scabbard, his field glasses, and a saddlebag of ammo, along with a saddlebag of pemmican and some jerky. They munched on it as they rode north.

"Why did they take Daisy and leave B.J.?" He asked her. Her dark eyes looked at the Crow riding ahead of them.

"A squaw probably told her man to bring her back a baby. Mebbe she lost hers. They left B.J. because he was still on his mother's milk." She said. "Daisy can eat most anyt'ing, now she has some first teeths."

Ben, thinking about it, decided she was right—-hoped she was. He kept thinking they might just ride up to a spot where the baby would be lying dead.

* * *

What they did ride up on was one of Ben's Percherons with its head down, shot in the paunch with an arrow, of which just the arrow fletches protruded. Ben cussed when he saw it. He knew every one of his horses and this one, "Old Charlie" had been a damn good horse in its day. Now, though, it evidently couldn't keep up the pace and the Blackfeet had arrowed it just out of spite. Ben rode up to it, got down and put his arms around the neck of the big horse and promised that he would kill a Blackfoot for what had been done to him, then shot it with his .45. The rage came back and he trembled as he got back aboard Snake.

12

They went on. Ben could tell from the considering looks he was getting from the Crow that they doubted the white man's ability to keep up with them. Some of them had snickered when they saw his mount. On the other hand, they had shown some admiration for Siccoolum's glossy black. They rode hard and the trail grew fresher. Night came and they didn't stop until just before dawn, to stretch, water the horses at a small spring and drink some hurried coffee that Siccoolum made, using it to wash down some jerky.

* * *

It was mid-morning of the second day, a fine sunny one, and they had followed the trail down off into the breaks that preceded the river, when they were held up by a round of fire coming from a bench to their front. Immediately, Many Coups gestured and Crow split off to either side.

Ben got down, led Snake into cover and looked through his glasses at the situation ahead. At the river, the Blackfeet were urging the big herd of horses across. About six hundred yards out from where he was observing, shots were coming from a little ring of rocks. As he watched, another shot rang out and with the glasses, he happened to see where it had come from: a boulder overlapped by a scrub cedar to the left of the center of the rocky face.

He threw Siccoolum his reins and pulling the Sharps from its scabbard, jacked in a shell as he took a seat behind a nut pine that afforded a good rest. Waiting, with his glasses in hand, he watched as the Crow worked towards the position from either side, while the bulk of the Crow kept a fire going to the front to keep the attention of the defenders centered there. Then he saw a flash of brown behind the rock and fired. Down there, an arm swung up and down again, and the spot was silent.

13

He swung over to another place where he'd seen a twinkle of something, maybe a piece of jewelry or a rifle barrel, and watched that location. An instant later, it flashed again and he put a bullet at it. A cry came back. Then, from the rocks, an Indian went running. Ben saw him as he was reloading and tracking him with his rifle barrel, was about to shoot, when he saw the brave go down, then get up again and hobble forward, shooting back as he limped along, trying to make it to where Ben now could see the heads of some horses tied behind trees. He was nearly to the animals when Ben fired, and the Indian tumbled.

The Crow were rushing forward from either side and the front one touched the fallen warrior with his coup stick, then crashed a tomahawk down into his head and began scalping the dead man.

The three had been sent back to provide a measure of time for the herd to get across the river and now, as the Crow party went forward, it could be seen that the end of the herd had already emerged from the water and was going up into the hills on the far side. On the near side, was another of Ben's Percherons—like Old Charlie, paunch shot with a protruding arrow. Ben killed it with his pistol, as he had done the first one, damning anyone who would do that to a horse. The last of the herd disappeared up through the bluffs, with several Blackfeet potting at them from positions on that side. Ben set up and threw some shots at them and the fire diminished.

The Crow stopped at the river's edge for a parley, surrounding Ben and Siccoolum, who started making a fire to brew a pot of coffee. She had tied a pot to her saddle and thrown in a sack of beans she had ground already, riding in a bag inside the pot. The fire going, she went to the river and dipped up some water, then came back and measured out the coffee and set it to boil. She stood and listened as Many Coups addressed her, in Crow and sign language, which she translated for Ben.

14

"He says to tell you that you did good shootin'. You are like they say, an eagle with a gun. He says he is sorry for our loss. Both our daughter and her man, and our big horses, which he see you loved."

Ben nodded his thanks, then said, "Tell him I am sad but I want revenge on the Blackfeet and won't rest until I see more of 'em over my gunsights."

Her hands flew and she spoke again. "He says we camp here to make them think we are quitting the trail. Then, we will follow the Blackfeet tonight. But that this ford is an ambush. There is another ford he knows up the river from here. We will go there when it's dark and cross, then take up their trail again. He thinks that they might have met up with some more Blackfeet or perhaps some Flathead, their friends, waiting here at the river. He says those you killed were Flathead, not Piegan." Many Coups held up a fresh scalp and grinned. He rattled Crow and threw some sign language.

"He says you shoot well. He wants you to have the first scalp." Ben nodded and took the grisly trophy, wishing it had been a Blackfoot. The coffee was smelling good. He handed it off to Siccoolum, who smiled and stuck it in her saddle bags.

* * *

That night, they took the trail again, going upriver for an hour, then striking across, following Many Coup's pinto as it hit the water and immediately began swimming in the deep current. Ben had never had Snake in the water and was anxious as to how the horse might take it, but he swam with a will, dragging Ben along behind him. Siccoolum's black up ahead was a water horse, too, but in back of him, he heard a slight commotion as one of the Crow had trouble, then a soft cry as man and horse went under.

Ben managed to turn Snake and just by luck, saw a body floating a few yards from him, the horse gone,

15

rolling away and under in the water's current. Snake struck out at Ben's urging and he came up to the figure as it went under again. Reaching down and grabbing it by the Crow's braids, he raised up and got the brave's head free of the water, then grasped it around the neck in an iron grip as he struggled to hold on to the tail and the brave, also.

Just when he was about to have to let go to save himself, Snake hit shallow water and Ben got his legs under him and dragged the Crow to the bank. He wasn't breathing and as the others gathered around, Ben pumped him up and down over a driftwood log, getting water to gush out of the man's mouth.

Abruptly, he coughed and choked, then began gasping in shallow heaves. Many Coups and another brave grasped him and got him to his feet, then walked him about for a while until he was fully conscious. Then the young brave came back to where Ben was standing and saying something, put his hand on Ben's chest. He signed and Siccoolum, standing near, translated,

"He says, 'He thanks you for his life. The Water Spirit had nearly taken him home to his lodge. His name is "Takes the Enemy's Gun" and he wants you to know that you and he are now brothers.'"

Ben was ready to mount and did so, saying,

"Tell him he is welcome. I give him his life back so that he may go with us to kill Blackfeet and their friends. Let's do it."

The party had taken the dead Flathead's horses and now a Crow brought up one for the rescued man to ride, handing him one of the guns taken, also. The party rode from the river, following Many Coups closely, as he again headed north.

* * *

Near dawn, with the sky lightening, Many Coups brought them to a halt, and they crowded up around him.

16

He pointed and Ben saw what he had seen. A small light flickered in the distance: a campfire with figures walking about it, making it appear and disappear.

The Crow war chief spoke low and Siccoolum whispered to Ben. "He says we must be careful. They will have eyes out. He will go with another wolf-scout and see how the camp lies."

Many Coups dismounted and the party made themselves comfortable, some chewing on jerky, some going off a little to take a leak or do their business, getting themselves ready for a fight. Some took out war paint and began making themselves up and several took the paint and put red hands on their horses or twined feathers in their manes.

Ben chewed a piece of jerky and waited. The sun was lightening the horizon when Many Coups and his fellow brave returned. He cleared a piece of ground and drew the camp, showing them where the horse herd was.

Ben asked, "Should we follow and wait to hit them tonight, does he think?" Siccoolum asked the question and Many Coups replied, as she told Ben,

"No, we must do it now. Their villages are not far off and then there would be too many to handle. As it is, they are double our number and it will be a fight. He asks, does the white man want to go with those who take the herd or with the rest, who will hit the camp?"

Ben said, "I don't have enough scalps yet, and we are still looking for Daisy, tell him. The baby is mainly why we are here, so it must be the camp."

He says, "It is good. You are a brave white man. He has seen only a few, he says."

Many Coups stood and rattled off orders and the men designated mounted their horses and headed off, evidently to take the herd. Then the rest, including Siccoolum and Ben, followed him.

17

Crow War Council

CHAPTER 3.

Many Coups' Crow struck the camp with a headlong charge that took the Blackfeet nearly by surprise, the drumming hooves alone alerting them that they were coming, when it was almost too late. Ben, on Snake, was at the front of the line as it swept in, shooting his Henry dry, then thrusting it beneath his leg and using his Colt as the battle degenerated into a dusty swirl of fighting whose participants were hard to distinguish as to foe or friend.

Siccoolum, as he'd told her, stuck close by him, using her short Colt with some effect, and they looked for little Daisy as they could, then she screamed at him and pointed. In the center of the camp, a brave was fighting, while on the ground by him was the baby. They headed over there, the Blackfoot engaged with a Crow in a hand-to-hand struggle with tomahawks and knives.

"Git Daisy!" Ben shouted and he spurred Snake over both fighters, locked together as they were, then shot the Blackfoot as he came up with his tomahawk to throw it. The Crow dived upon the brave as he went down and nearly beheaded him with his weapon, then with a scream, took his scalp and headed back into the battle.

Ben turned back and Siccoolum had scooped up the baby, which was crying lustily. Ben watched closely as the battle raged about them, using his bullets with care to keep her and the baby safe as he could, reloading when there was a lull. They kept their horses between them and the fight as much as possible, and soon, under Many Coups' fierce and canny leadership and fighting skill, saw the battle turn in the Crow favor. The Blackfeet and the Flatheads with them began a fighting withdrawal, those who were left. The Crow relentlessly kept after them, screaming their war cries, and the battle moved into the timber, where the Blackfeet melted away.

Ben got down and checked to see that his charges were okay. Siccoolum was talking low to the bundle in her arms and Ben saw that the baby, hearing the familiar voice, had quieted. Both were unhurt and Ben heaved a sigh of relief.

He looked about him. The camp was littered with dead and a few wounded, and the Crow were dispatching them as he watched. Lying near him was a Crow, shot in the chest. He went to him and saw it was Takes The Enemy's Gun. The wound was a lung shot, and he lifted the young man up and turned him slightly so that the wound was out of the dirt. The man's eyes opened. Ben nodded his head and something made him fasten his gaze upon the brave's eyes as he put his hand against the wound. He pushed hard and the man exhaled. Ben spoke to him.

Encouraged, the injured man took a deep breath and dark blood gouted out in a torrent, then began a steady pulsing of red. Seeing that, Ben called to Siccoolum and she found a dead brave with a buckskin shirt, which she cut off and brought to him. He used a portion of it to make two pads, which he covered the front and back openings with, then wrapped the remainder around the chest and tied it tightly, sealing the wounds. Then Ben got the man onto his feet and began walking him to and fro, talking, encouraging him as he went.

While he was engaged in this, Siccoolum was up to her usual, scalping dead Blackfeet and Flatheads who were lying about with their hair yet. Once, he saw her use her knife on a wounded brave, cutting his throat as he tried feebly to stop her.

"Bloodthirsty little witch." He muttered. She held the dead brave's scalp up for him triumphantly as he watched her, shaking his head.

* * *

Many Coups presently returned, himself covered with blood, packing several scalps. He saw Ben holding up the young warrior and went to them. Taking the man in his arms, he sat him down and as the other Crow came up and began looking for their wounded or dead, Many Coups spoke to Takes the Enemy's Gun, who responded coherently. What he said made Many Coups take a hard look at Ben.

He gave orders and they made preparations to leave, gathering guns and other weapons, bringing up horses. Two braves brought a gentle horse up and they made a travois out of blankets from the battle litter for Takes the Enemy's Gun and laid him on it, tying him there. Ben saw the brave's eyes were on him and waved encouragingly.

One of his friends started off right away with the horse following and Ben looking, saw that there were three more treated likewise, plus several dead tied on their horses. Then Many Coups waved his arm and they began, following the trail of the large horse herd. Many Coups rode beside Ben, talking to him and then using sign, as Siccoolum, following, translated again.

"He says you killed many with your shooting. He rode close by and saw you. He says he is glad we found the baby. I tell him it is all right. He says you took Takes His Enemy's Gun's spirit in your hands today, as you did

21

last night. He asks if you are a medicine man of your people. What shall I tell him?" He glanced at her and saw she was solemn.

"Tell him 'no.' Just a man who has seen many battles and knows a little about wounds." What she really said made Ben wonder, though, for Many Coups eyed him intently, then kneed his horse and went off to check on the horse herd up ahead.

* * *

They caught up to the herd as they hit the river again, using the ford they had crossed the night before. He was relieved to see Atlas in the bunch and making his way to the big horse after the crossing, saw that he was unharmed. Siccoolum sighted her buckskin and cut it out, putting her rope on it with no Crow objecting. Ben, now that he'd seen Atlas, was content to let the rest of the herd go along with their new captors. He glimpsed the Perkins stud, too, then later caught sight of the trader's mare.

He dropped back to check how Takes the Enemy's Gun was getting along and was happy to see the man raise his hand and wave. A lung shot was bad but he'd seen men survive such a wound. Maybe this young brave would. He hoped so.

* * *

They weren't followed, although Many Coups sent men to watch their back trail. The morning of the third day after the battle, they were home and the Crow held the herd while he and Many Coups cut their stock off and ran it into the corral below the big house. Freddy came running as they streamed into the place, yelling. Siccoolum rode up to the house and handed Daisy down to Betty, who took

22

the little girl into her arms and with Katy, brought her into the house to be cleaned up and attended to.

Many Coups came and asked Ben if the wounded might be housed in the barn until they died or healed enough to travel. Ben agreed readily, saying they would care for them. The men had endured a torturous two days to get there and one had died enroute. The dead one had not been Takes His Enemy's Gun, though, and for that, Ben was thankful. They unloaded them and made them comfortable in the sweet hay in the barn, bringing them water and food from the house at Ben's directions.

"I will leave the other white men's horses here with you to do as you wish." Many Coups said. "You fought for them. You should keep them, is my thinking." He held out his hand and Ben gripped it. This was a man he would fight beside again, each felt.

"We'll see. That isn't the white man's way. I want to say, Many Coups, that you and your Crow are welcome any time to my fire."

"You must come and visit our people, BenHite, the man who the Bannacks call "Faraway Gun," the man who kills from a distance. And your fighting Gros Ventre squaw!"

Siccoolum, translating this, had the grace to at least look down in confusion. The war chief left some of the wounded men's friends to care for them, and the Crow went on, after being fed.

23

Wild Rose

CHAPTER 4.

Kittledge and Ketchum had attended to the burials, fencing a small plot on a near hillside overlooking the creek. Ben found some flat granite and carved headstones that he erected over the graves. The girls transplanted some wild roses and purple prairie clover into the plot and Ketchum made a nice arch over the gate.

In due time, Reed and Bowles came to claim their property. They looked askance at whether Ben would try to retain their horses, as it was unwritten custom among the Indians for ownership to transfer to those who had recovered the property, or at least make the owner cough up a payment. Ben surprised them by letting them take them all, even the mare and the stud, which was their main concern. The friendly feeling that engendered prompted Major Reed to say,

"You're being big-hearted about this, Hite. Ya know what store we put by the mare, let alone the stud. So maybe I kin pay you back a little. Me an' J.J. heard awhile back about yore set-to with the Mormons and the reward they had out on you. We was kinda thinkin' we might try to take 'em up on it, 'cause, ya know, $5000 is alot of money, but now, why, we'll just forget that idee and I want to say, that if we hear of anyone snoopin' 'round to try fer it, we'll either take keer of it ourselves or give you word."

He held out his dirty hand and Ben shook it, reflecting that he needed the good feelings of his neighbors, even if he didn't like them much.

* * *

The wounded Crow were no problem. Their friends settled them in the barn and went out and killed some deer and a cow elk and they feasted on that and the soups Siccoolum brought them. Each of the injured men wanted Ben to put his hands on the wound after Takes the Enemy's Gun told them how he had helped save him. He did so. Waterwheel helped his mother and with the others chipping in at times, soon, one by one, the men healed and left for home. Last was Takes the Enemy's Gun and he was healed for a time before he finally left, with his eyes toward Katy, who didn't encourage him, Ben felt. That relieved him. He couldn't see her in a smoky tipi.

* * *

Now Siccoolum had her heart's wish: babies of her own to take care of. B.J. and Daisy were cuddled and spoiled, though B.J. was a problem, being still on mother's milk. They had no cows that were fresh and he rejected much of the food that Siccoolum chewed for him, in the Indian way.

The Metis came to visit and solved that right away, as one of the women had just been delivered of a new baby herself and had milk enough for the little boy, too. That meant, though, that he would have to go to their camp and Betty surprised Ben at least, when she volunteered to take the boy and care for him while they were there. He gave his consent and she packed some clothes and cheerfully went with Louie and his wife to the Metis, packing B.J. in a back cradle Siccoolum had made for him. Ben felt there was something there he was missing but he couldn't see what it was, so dismissed it.

26

He was occupied with strengthening their defenses and had decided to employ a couple men just to act as guards. In the back of his mind, he was still thinking the Mormons were a threat, let alone another war party. Using some reinforced wagon jacks, he lifted the house Moira and Miles had lived in, put it on skids and using his teams, pulled it up and over the hill to a new spot close in to the stables, making a partial enclosure. Ketchum and his new bride soon came to occupy the home. After he had moved it, though, Ben regreted it, because every time he looked at it from the porch, he thought of the night he'd found Moira in it.

* * *

The three Mormon kids had adapted into the family well. Tommy and Brigham, like Waterwheel, were typical boys and after Ben showed them how to catch grasshoppers or dig worms and present them to the hungry trout in the cold spring creek, they had more fish than they could eat at times. He took them hunting, too, and Tommy shot his first deer with Ben's repeater. After that, Waterwheel and Brigham clamored for guns, and Ben obliged them, thinking that the sooner they learned to shoot, the better for the defense of the place. He liked the new Winchesters, which were a distinct improvement over the more fragile Henrys, and bought all three boys the new '73 carbines in .44 WCF. Lakey brought them out from Fort Benton and they were early Christmas presents, as Ben wanted to get the boys used to the guns as quickly as he could.

Abigail was some help in the house with the younger babies and soon was over her homesickness, with so much going on. The other kids didn't treat her any different and she soon found her place at the table and fed herself, too.

* * *

For some time, Siccoolum had been bothered with a cough that had gotten gradually worse. To Ben, an old hand at sickness since he'd seen so much during the war, it didn't sound good, deep in her chest. She dismissed it, working as hard as ever, but he managed to take some of the burden off her shoulders, employing Ketchum's wife at the house. It didn't help. He could see she was growing weak. So he decided to use an excuse to go into Fort Benton to see if the Mormons had done as he instructed them, to take her to the new doctor there, whom Lakey said had a good reputation.

* * *

They rode in followed by a freight wagon driven by Freddy, with Katy in attendance. Kittledge and Bless stayed back to manage things, with Felice and another Metis woman to take care of the house and kids and do the chores. Bless had also brought two of the young Metis' over to function as guards while Ben and Freddy were gone, so his mind was relieved on that point.

At the river opposite the town, they crossed on a new ferry there which accommodated the wagon and the horses easily. Once there, he checked them into the pretentious new brick hotel, which stood right by the river. When the officious clerk saw Siccoolum come through the door, he came from behind his counter and tried to shoo her out, saying,

"Get out! No Indians allowed in here! Go on!"

Ben stepped in front of him and said in a low tone, "That <u>Indian</u> is my wife! You'll treat her as such, by God!"

The clerk took one look at Ben's set face and stepped back behind his counter, saying, "Of course, Sir. I didn't know. It's just we have a rule..."

Ben turned and saw that she had disappeared. He went out and found her by the river bank. Though she

28

protested, he led her back in and taking the key from the sullen clerk, they trooped upstairs. Once there, he ordered baths for them all, to get rid of the trail dust. The water was cold when it came and Ben stormed downstairs. Grabbing the clerk by his shirt front, he drew him up tight across the counter and said,

"Listen, you sonovabitch! I'm paying fer some service here and I expect it to be first class! Now, you git to carrying water up that stairs fer us and it goddamn sure better be hot! <u>DO</u> I make myself clear?"

The clerk's face was white and he nodded his head vigorously as behind them, a voice drawled,

"Damn, Ben! I do believe that's the first time I seen you lose that temper of yours since the war!"

Turning, he saw Hank and Will, all dressed to the hilt, Will carrying a fancy cane. They were both grinning at his display of anger.

"Well...Hello, boys."

He let go of the man's shirt and grabbed their hands, shaking and slapping their shoulders in delight. He hadn't seen them for weeks and had often wondered how they might be doing.

"Having some trouble with the service in this pile of bricks, Ben?" Will asked. The gaudy pretentiousness of the hotel didn't impress either of the men too much. They had seen the best establishments of New York, Boston St. Louis and other eastern cities and beside them, the Grande Hotel of Fort Benton cut a small figure.

"That fart in the wind was giving me shit because I brought Siccoolum into their Goddamn high falutin' gilded outhouse!"

"Yep, you'll find that kind of thinkin' is on display in just about every business here, except the ones that want their money or their furs. The bars don't want them, neither do the rest of the shops. But they'll sell 'em rotgut out the back. The drunk ones that hang around town <u>can</u> be a real nuisance, though."

"Siccoolum <u>isn't</u> a drunk Injun! She's my wife. I married her in front of a priest." Ben grated.

"I know, old friend, but they don't know that. However, you keep hoorahing the help and they damn sure will find out." Hank said with a smile. "Why don't you let Will and I treat you all to some supper? They have a good restaurant here. And a bar."

"Sounds good, but we just got in and I want a bath and then I need to find a good doctor."

Hank raised his eyebrows. "You don't look sick. Is it one of the kids?"

"Nope. It's her. She's got a cough that I don't much care for."

"Hmmm." A look passed between them. Ben and the two men knew well that a deep persistent cough could mean consumption, a lung disease that was likely fatal. They'd seen too much of it, had lost too many friends from it. During the war, more men were lost to sickness than to battle.

"Doc Sandstrom two blocks down is the one I'd take her to, but he's busy. You may need an appointment to get her in to him. And he might be of the same mind as some of the businesses as to treating an Indian."

Hank saw his friend's face cloud over again and spread his hands. "Ben, I'm on your side. I'm just telling you so that you can be forewarned."

"I know, but she...Damn it, Hank, she's saved my life——more'n once! She's fought beside me! I got to tell you about the scrape we had three weeks ago with a Blackfoot war party that killed Moira and Miles an' gathered up half the horses in the Territory, including the Crow! She was right there and a lot of help to us. I'm worried about her and I damn sure won't see her put down by any smarmy shithead."

He was still steaming and the sight of the man going up the stairs packing two pails of hot water didn't cool him down much. Taking a close look at the cut of his two friends, he asked,

"You boys look pretty swell fer a couple buff hunters. What's doin'?"

Hank and Will preened a little, like two peacocks,

"Why, Ben, we took our hide money and bought an interest in a steamer with a friend of ours. It made two trips up this summer and got us a pot full of dollars. Capt'n Saunders of the *Elena* let us in. He's a hell of a riverman, knows it like the back of his hand."

"Steamboats! Hell!" Ben turned to go back upstairs. "See you at supper!"

"Drag us out of the bar," Will said as they headed for that establishment through the swinging doors. Inside, the familiar smell of whiskey, beer and tobacco rolled over them like a welcoming fog, one they both embraced.

Upstairs, Ben saw that Siccoolum had taken her bath and left the water for him. He looked at the dirt ring around the tub and called down for new water, which the clerk brought on the run.

* * *

The supper that night was a fine affair, with Ben loosening up a little when he managed to pull his two comrades from the saloon and set them down for a good meal, which made him even more relaxed. Will was drunk and Hank nearly so and they alternated between stories and Will's poetry, which was something to hear, even to the *Mormon's Lament*, which Ben tried without success, to squelch. Katy and Freddy listened wide-eyed as Hank told about the man they called "Father Ben" and the war, and Will chimed in with his own episodes. Siccoolum listened without comment, uneasy in the white man's establishment and too tense not to show it, though Ben constantly tried to reassure her. She ate little, he saw.

31

The doctor the next day, listened to Ben's description of Siccoolum's cough and his fears, then asked her to come in to be examined. That took much persuasion on Ben's part, and almost resulted in a wrestling match there in the anteroom before he corralled her into the examining room for the doctor to take a look at her. The stethoscope he used to listen to her heart and lungs scared her, too, but the physician, a gray headed elderly gentleman with a pointed goatee and kind eyes behind strong glasses, had a good manner about him and he settled her down so that she became obedient to his instructions, taking deep breaths when he told her, turning from side to side.

Out in his office later, he gave Ben the bad news.

"Your suspicions were correct, I'm afraid. Consumption, or medically, Pulmonary Tuberculosis. A particularly virulent disease of the lungs. In her case, I wouldn't give her but another month or two before....Well, I wish I was wrong, but I saw too many such cases during the War. I'm sorry, Mr. Hite."

"Christ, Doc! She's a young woman yet. You're dead positive?"

"Certain as the sun will come up tomorrow, Sir. It hits our savage brethern very hard as they seem to have little physical defense against such white man's diseases. Even measles kills them. All I can recommend is bed rest and warmth. Keep her clean and be sure to burn any blood or sputum—spit— she might expel. Clean her eating utensils with alcoholic spirits. We learned during the war that alcohol has a cleansing effect, for some reason."

Ben was stunned. "What do I owe you?"

"$10 will cover it. Again, I want to express my sincere condolences. She seems a....nice young woman."

"Doc, you don't know the half of it." Ben turned away before the man saw the tears in his eyes.

* * *

Their return to the ranch was a subdued affair. Somehow, without Ben telling them, the others were aware that Siccoolum was deathly sick. Siccoolum herself, said nothing. Ben had the feeling that she already knew.

Missouri in flood stage

CHAPTER 5.

"I want to die outside, with Sun on my face."

She was in the bedroom upstairs, where she'd been lying for nearly a month. Ben had attended her through her sickness the whole time, with help from Katy, though he was afraid she might contract the sickness, so he'd not let her do much. She had her hands full downstairs with Daisy, the household and cooking, anyway, though Felice was helping, too.

Siccoolum was silent most of the time, never complaining, though Ben knew it hurt her to breathe and tried to help as he could, even spoon feeding her as she got weaker and helping her when she needed the bed pan. He kept her clean and stayed with her constantly. She seemed content to just have him near, and asked continually about the children, who talked to her through the doorway often, the threshold being as far as Ben would let them come.

Now it was March and a warm sun was shining through the window, with spring not far away. In the trees outside, he could hear some of the returning birds through the partially open window. He sat in his usual place, a chair right beside her bed. He caught her hand as she tried to raise it, bringing it to his face and letting the tears flow over their entwined fingers.

"I want to be buried the old way, in a tree or a picane (scaffold) above the ground, facing Sun, where Our Father Spirit lives. I wish you believed that, too, so that

35

you would come to me later in the Shadow Land. You have been good to me, Ben Hite, and I tried to be a wife who took care of her brave warrior. My Eagle with a gun, as the Crow chief said. I just wish...we could have had some little ones of our own." She squeezed his hand. "Now you must remember our happy times."

Her hand dropped from his, and he tucked the mutilated member under the covers with a pat.

"Siccoolum...Luv...you were—are, the best wife and woman a man could have. I will try to find you in the Shadow Land! This I swear."

He carried her down the stairs and out the door, to the porch, and put her in his big chair. Covering her with a robe, he went back in to get her some coffee, which she loved. When he came back, she was gone.

* * *

Her funeral was attended by the Metis, the traders and several white incomers to the Basin, curious as to what was happening and hoping for a party. After all, it was just a dead Indian squaw.

Ben asked Father Dupree to say some words over her, which he obligingly did. Ben thanked them all for coming, then took her down to the barn and ran in the horses, choosing Monte to ride. He saddled her black with her self-made saddle, the horse shying at her body as it lay there. The buckskin, though, stood steady. He climbed aboard Monte, then had Freddy hand her up to him, the youngster crying unashamedly.

Walking Monte slowly, he led the other horses over the trail east toward the Moccasins, up into the pines, to an open ledge of rock high up that he had thought about which was secluded enough to give her some privacy. Dismounting awkwardly, he set her down gently beneath a tree. Then taking his axe, he cut down some cedars and fashioned a platform to hold her body, lifted her up and

36

placed her there, wrapped in two good buffalo robes with her carbine by her side, her pistol and some shells in her elk skin skirt pocket, her knives in her belt, and some sacks of pemmican and candy by her side to feed her on her journey.

Then he led the two horses to the scaffold, and with an apology to them on his lips, shot them both, laying them down at the bottom of the platform, so that she might have horses to ride when she went on the journey to the Shadow Land.

He stood there for a long while, then, and watched the sun go down. It was dark before he climbed wearily on Monte and walked him down the trail to home.

PART II

Courtesy of Jody Menge

CHAPTER 6.

Now the family began to unravel like an old rope. Waterwheel was set on leaving after his mother died. Ben caught him saddling his horse. Asking him where he was going, the boy replied that Takes his Enemy's Gun had told him he was welcome at his fire in the Crow village on the Bighorn. He wanted to go, was going to go, was an Indian, not a white man, and after some fruitless arguing, Ben gave him his grulla and two other horses, weapons, some money and traveling gear and let him go on his way, wondering if he had done the right thing. He wondered what Siccoolum would have said. The boy had hugged him there at the last and told him he'd liked having him as a father, but he had to go.

* * *

Betty came home with a hulking young Metis', who had come to ask him for her hand. The young girl was glowing now with advanced pregnancy, and Ben saw little else he could do than give his consent and wish them well. Jacques Blaquet was a question. He wouldn't meet Ben's eyes. His own deep, close-set eyes and ridged shelf for a forehead presented a formidable aspect. He wouldn't have been a choice, or even in the running for Betty, had Ben anything to say about it. He suited Betty, though, and she asked if she might keep B.J., which took a burden off young Katy. Ben agreed with some conditions.

He went with them to see the land Jacques had picked out and it was a favorable piece of bottom land along the Judith River, with a small shack already up. He'd started a garden the year before and proudly showed Ben how he planned to extend it and put additional acres under plow when he could. Ben went home trying to get his mind around it.

* * *

Freddy was wanting to go with Lakey the next time he came through. Steele had offered him a job and he had asked Ben if he minded if he went. Ben wondered why everyone wanted to leave suddenly.

* * *

Katy brought him a cup of coffee as he sat there on the porch and he asked her to sit with him. She plumped down with a sigh and sipped on a cup of tea and he said,

"So, Honey, Waterwheel has sloped off to the Crow. Your little sis has gone and got herself married to a Metis'. She wants to keep B.J. Freddy has asked me if he can go off with Lakey, freighting. What do you want to do? Leave me, too?"

She got up and put her arms around his neck and hugged him. "We all love you, Father Ben. But you knew it would happen, sooner or later."

He grasped her hands.

"I know, Honey. It's life, I guess. But I'm askin' you, what do you want to do?" The question made her eyes glow and he reflected that she was growing into a beautiful woman. He thought not for the first time that he would have liked to have glimpsed their mother. She had to have been a handsome woman.

40

"I'd like to go to school. Back east somewhere."

The answer didn't surprise him too much. She had always had a bent toward learning.

"What can a girl learn at school? What good is it? A woman doesn't have many jobs open to her, even back east, Honey."

"I know. There isn't much a woman can do on her own, except house maid, wash clothes or teach. But...I'd like to study medicine. I still remember a story you told us about a woman named Barton who helped nurse you when you were wounded in the war. I see a need for it, Father, especially with women like Siccoolum, who was scared of a male doctor."

She laughed self-consciously. "I'm sure most women would rather have a female doctor than a man."

Ben shook his head, "I doubt that any medical school back east would accept a woman, Honey. Men run the world. But it's a good idea. A woman doctor for women makes sense, all right."

It was a good idea, he mused. If they could find a medical school that would let her study. If she could get a degree. If she could get some state to give her a license. She had a good head on her. He had the money to make it happen, maybe. And he needed to make a trip back east, anyway, back to Arkansas, where the Perkins train had originated. And to see if his mother was still living. Maybe she needed some help, since the War.

"Let me think on it, Hon. There's Daisy and the rest of the kids, you know."

* * *

He had taken time on the trip to Benton to go to the Wells Fargo bank and he'd found that his account had been fattened by $40,000 from Rawls, $100,000 from the Bank of Zion, and $15,000 from Owens. He was rich by any standard of the day, since he already had over $45,000

41

in the bank there already. The president, a starchy little wisp of a man with glasses that made him look like an owl, had all but gotten down to shine his boots when he'd found out who he was.

But all that money hadn't kept Siccoolum alive. The scaffold that held her up to the Sun and the weather kept intruding into his thoughts at random times of the day. The dead horses lying under it. Good ones. 'Should he have killed them?'

Katy went inside and he sat and thought, looking out at Moira-Ketchum's house, then on across the bench over to the wooded ridge. Behind it was the rock ledge where Sicoolum rested. He closed his eyes.

'Too many memories here,' he thought.

About then, Abigail came and clambered up on his lap. From the barn came Tommy with little Brig in tow. They'd finished helping Kittledge and Ketchum with the horses and the milking, and Tommy was carrying a heavy milk bucket to run through the separator Ben had brought from Benton. The kids were laughing about something Kittledge had said. First, he thought, he needed to do something about them. He remembered back to that night that Moira and Miles had died—that supper had been so good, they'd had so much fun. 'Christ! Goddam it! Life hurt!'

* * *

Freddy went with Steele before the week was out, and he took half of the Percherons with him. Ben had given the horses to Freddy, to bring into the partnership he and Steele had, with the idea that the boy would take Ben's side of it over one day. Ben had talked with Lakey and the man was willing to take the youngster in hand. He was glad to have the new horses, too, as his business had expanded. Of the draft horses, that left the team Ketchum wanted, a team for Jacques and Betty, for a wedding

42

present, Kittledge's two teams and Atlas and some mares in the pasture.

* * *

"Where we goin', Father Ben?"

Abigail was sitting in the second seat of the carriage Ben had found and bought in Helena after taking the kids horseback to the city. Brigham's son was a good rider, but Abigail was just too young yet to chance on a horse by herself, consequently, she'd had to ride the whole way either in front or behind Ben and it got to be torture for them both, as she'd grown.

They had stayed over at the best hotel in the city, the Strathmore, while she recuperated a little and Ben went looking for a light buggy. He found instead a well sprung carriage for sale and bought it. Then, he needed a good team and that took another day of looking before he came to a livery on the outskirts of town that had what he was looking for: a mature, matched pair of good-looking bays that cost him four hundred dollars, a high figure even in that gold rich city.

With polished harness, the horses shod for the road and groomed, the new conveyance was a fine sight. It even had a rain cover, in case of weather. Ben brought a fine buffalo robe for the kids to bundle under if they got cold, filled the back with their gear and getting up on the driver's seat, they were off. Tommy followed behind with the other horses.

He hadn't told them where he was taking them when they had left the ranch, but after having them tell Kittledge, Ketchum and Katy 'goodbye' Tommy had an inkling. He said to Ben, as they were in the barn saddling the horses,

"I don't <u>want</u> to go back to Utah! I want to stay with you!" He came and grabbed onto Ben, hugging him. Hite was touched and he gave the boy a hug in return.

43

"Son, I like having you here. You bin a lot of help and I appreciate it. I intend to pay you some wages fer the work you did, too. But things have changed since Siccoolum left us. Your Dad paid some big money on his debt to me and it's just right that I take you kids home. The little ones need their folks and it's just not right to keep 'em any longer."

"Kin I come back later, maybe?"

"Sure thing, son...but I may not be here."

* * *

Now Ben answered truthfully, "I'm taking you kids home, Honey."

"Will you stay, too? I want you to stay, too, Father Ben!"

"No, Hon, I can't. Katy and Atlas would miss me. 'Sides, your Ma and Dad'll be there. They bin missin' you."

"I know, but I wish you would stay with us. I feel safe when you're with us."

"Me, too, Please stay with us, Father Ben." Brigham Jr. pleaded.

Ben was touched and despite himself, ended up assuring them he would come and visit them, though he wondered how he'd make that happen.

* * *

They made good time on what was now a well-traveled road, putting up at Butte, then Dillon, then on to Lima and over the pass, through to Idaho falls and Pocatello, and finally to Corinne, Logan and on into Salt Lake City.

They put up at the Englewood Inn, a comfortable hotel with a good livery. He used a different name and kept the kids quiet in their room. Ben was amazed at how the

44

city had built up and spread up the valley. The Mormon cult was prospering. He fed the children a grand meal that night, gave Tommy a sizable sum for his work, then in the morning, after a good breakfast, took them out to Owens' farm. Torry's wives were in the kitchen and came running out when they drove up. Tommy's mother screamed when she saw him, and began crying. That got the other women going and soon, Abigail began. But she clung to Ben when he tried to hand her down to the Owens women.

"Here's the kids. Return Young's two fer me. Tommy, the horse you're riding is yours. The other's for Brigham, here. Come 'ere and shake my hand, boys."

Tommy did more than that, crying now, too, and hugging Ben, which made Brigham and Abigail cling to him, also.

The women were puzzled—-wasn't this the murdering kidnapper who had killed so many men? How could the kids be so sorry to see him leave? And was that a tear in the man's eye? Couldn't be.

* * *

Going back into the city, he managed to sell the carriage and flashy team at the livery for just a little less than he had paid for it. Then, leading Snake and the pack horses, headed out of town. As he passed by, he resolutely refused to look at the place where he and Siccoolum had lived, where his horses and stables had burned. His one hope now, he thought, was to sweep his mind clear of bad memories, as he had the War. This place was one of them.

It would have been bad for any Mormons who tried to take him, just then.

Photo courtesy of Bob Cherry

CHAPTER 7.

On a warm day in June, Kittledge drove Ben and Katy in to Benton in the buckboard behind another matched pair of young horses he was working for a light road team.

"How long you expect to be gone, Boss?"

"It'll be awhile, fer sure. Back east to git Katy settled, then out to Arkansas to try to find out who all are left from the Perkins people. Over to my old home place, maybe—- after that, I'm not sure, Kit."

"What all you want me 'n Bless to git done while you're gone?"

"Just keep the place up. Hev Felice take good care of Daisy. Take care of Atlas and his brood. Do the haying. Hire the Metis, if you need to. I should be back by Fall. You got your wages ahead an' I'm goin' to give you and Bless access to an account I'll start for the ranch at the bank. If you need anythin', just draw on it. And stay alert."

"You kin count on us, Boss."

"I know I can, Kitt.....An' I'm grateful."

* * *

He and Katy walked aboard the *Nellie Peck* for the downriver voyage. The mile long levy at Benton had only four boats moored there when they had arrived and they had been lucky to get cabins for the downriver journey.

47

Ben had taken two for them and since the *Nellie Peck* had an experienced captain, Grant Marsh, of *Far West* fame, which he and Durfee owned also, the voyage promised to be a fast and safe one.Marsh, to Ben's knowledge, had never wrecked a boat.

The *Nellie Peck* was carrying forty-four passengers and 300 tons of freight, including some gold locked in the captain's safe. The freight was mainly bales of buffalo hides. These bales usually were ten hides pressed into a pack and tightly tied. Each weighed about two hundred pounds and it usually took two men to handle them down into the hold or stack them on deck. Ben noticed, though, a muscular black man of very large proportions who could take the bales and put them over his head, with no apparent struggle or stress.

The man had a sunny disposition, was always smiling. Ben, sipping coffee as he sat on a deck bench, liked to listen to the men as they sang together at the end of the day, after supper. The big darkie's deep bass voice underscored the river songs and made the windows vibrate with its tone. Captain Marsh encouraged the sing-a-longs with tots of whiskey to keep the passengers entertained. Ben suspected he, himself, liked to hear the music. Several of the crew could play an instrument, too, a couple pretty well. He knew from experience that on the Mississippi boats it was common for the bigger ones to employ whole bands and groups of entertainers. Here on the Missouri, though, it usually wasn't done. There weren't enough passengers to justify the expense. Cargo was king.

* * *

A week down the swollen river with a couple groundings on sandbars the only incident to hold the boat up, they came to Fort Union and pulled into the bank there. Since the demise of the beaver trade, the discovery of gold and the war, the fort had lost much of its importance but boats still stopped to take on freight, furs, skins, fresh meat, usually buffalo or elk, and discharge or take on passengers. The boat's purser announced a two hours delay while they loaded. The day was a warm, sunny one and it invited a walk on the shore.

Ben had not visited the historic place and he and Katy took the opportunity to tour the interior, seeing the Factor's house inside the enclosed walls, the stores and the warehouses that made up the fort. It teemed with men—-trappers, Indians, fort employees, and rivermen. There were few women, and those mainly squaws of the lower, slutty type that their men sold for money or whiskey.

Seeing the squalor and the drunken men and whores, Ben was sorry he'd taken Katy to the place and they turned to go back to the boat. He wasn't really surprised when their way was contested by a group of tipsy trappers. They were led by a tall French Canadien who wore buckskins like the others but had a bright red sash wrapped about his middle, from which protruded the handle of a pistol on the right side and a large knife scabbard on the left. He had a bottle in his hand and took a drink from it, then threw it towards the river and whooped like an Indian, doing a little jig, jumping from one foot to the other as he came forward and stood, weaving a little as he grinned with a drunken leer at Katy, ignoring Ben.

"Ah, It's a petite cherie, a little dove of rare beauty from the steamer! Tooot! Tooot! I fall, boys! I am in love!" He got down on one knee and spread his arms to her, nearly falling as he swayed..

Ben grinned, "No, just drunk, Frenchie. Dance along now and let us by, like the gentlemen I'm sure you boys are."

His easy demeanor in the face of what for most would be an intimidating situation, made them take a second look at the man before them. Their leader, though, was not to be put off. He had seen in the young woman to his front, something he thought he'd had been looking for all his life, a desirable young white female, likely a virgin, not a dirty poule like those who populated the tipis about the fort. Now he too, focused on Ben.

"You are...?" He was sobering up quickly, Ben saw, and maybe not as drunk as he let on.

"Her father, Frenchie, and real particular about who I let associate with my daughter. Now, I asked you polite-like to let us be. We need to git on back to the boat."

He started forward and the Frenchman stood his ground. Ben walked into him and gave him a shove that threw him into his friends behind him and the whole lot staggered, one falling back on his butt.

Frenchie's eyes got wide and he jumped forward, hissing at the insult, drawing his knife with a smooth motion as he came. Ben, though, was ready and his own blade was out in his hand. The sight caused the Frenchman to stop:—-that, and the sight of Ben grinning.

Then from the steamer came the boat's hands, led by the big black man. They were carrying axes and clubs and made a daunting sight as they formed up beside Ben.

In his deep voice, the darkie, the one they called "Big Harp" said, "Mistah Hite, Capt'n Marsh says to tell youse that we's ready to leave. You ready, sah?"

"Well now, this Frenchie thinks he wants to mess with me, Harp. The party's just started." Ben chuckled. Like the French trappers, Harp and the crew took a second look at a man who could laugh while a man with a knife was threatening him.

Seeing the resolute array of men facing them, the trappers made off like errant children, whooping and ki-yiing. Their leader smiled and bowed, a mocking salute to Ben, then kissed his hand and blew the kiss toward Katy, who blushed. He turned and followed his men and Ben couldn't resist saying, "Bye now, Frenchie!"

They turned and the hands followed them to the boat and up the gang plank. Captain Marsh was there waiting for them. He was solemn as he said,

"Thought I'd better send some hands over when I saw you having trouble with those voyageurs. Drunk, weren't they? Hope they didn't bother you or upset your daughter, sir."

"Just some boys on a spree, looking fer some excitement." Ben commented. Katy's face was still white, however. Marsh, like his hands, took another look at Ben. This man seemed a cool customer.

"I'm going to talk to the Company, anyway, about them letting the boats passengers be harassed. It's happened before and I've had enough of it."

"Suit yourself, Captain. But no harm done."

"Huh! I saw the knives. Looks like there could have been!"

Later, in the cabin, Katy said,

"I thought I was going to have to pull out my pistol!"

Ben had given her a small Colt pocket pistol which a gunsmith had converted to .32 cartridges. He had told her to carry it in her purse for "emergencies." "So, Father, was that an emergency?"

Ben laid down on the bed and said, "Guess it could have been. Never hurts to be ready, Honey. Now, I'm going to take a little nap before the supper bell rings."

"I'm not sleepy. But do you mind if I just stay here and sit and watch the loading? My cabin isn't so interesting, being on the other side." Her cabin faced the river, and though both had windows, hers usually looked out on the water, instead of into shore.

"Sure, Honey."

She was seated at the window when a shot came crashing through, throwing glass on her and missing her by just a few inches. She screamed and Ben jumped off

51

the bed, and grabbing her, took her to the floor of the cabin. "You hit, baby?"

She felt herself over. "No, but I've got glass in my hair!" She also had a small cut on her face from the flying shards. He looked at it and bringing a wet towel from the stand, gave it to her as he looked out the shattered window. He couldn't see anyone suspicious. "Did you see who it was?"

"It was the Frenchman you were arguing with. I saw him raise a rifle and shoot! I was frozen. I should have ducked."

"You're damn lucky he didn't kill you." Ben said as he reached under his bed and got his Henry from its case. He checked the loads and then pulled his Colt from under his coat and checked it, also. Then he turned to her, handing her his wallet.

"I'm going after him. You take this and if I don't come back, go to the captain and tell him what happened. The money in here will get you back home and you can think what to do, then, with Bless and Kitt."

"Dad! Don't go! There's too many of them! Don't leave me alone!"

"Have to, Honey. Nobody shoots at me or mine without I hit them back. Just the way I am." He went out.

Big Harp was carrying a bale of furs aboard when Ben went storming down the gangplank. He'd heard the shot but didn't connect it with the incident that had occurred earlier. Shots around the fort were common. He watched as Ben strode away.

He dropped the bale and motioning to a couple of the men working there to come with him, grabbed up an axe from the rack. The others did the same, wondering what was going on. Ben had already disappeared in the crowd on shore. Harp broke into a run.

Ben, going on shore, had glimpsed the Frenchman just going around a corner of the fort wall. He levered a shell in as he went faster, jogging as he went around the corner after him. Perhaps that was what the Frenchman wanted, for they were waiting there for him. He was standing in front of six of the trappers, congregated there with rifles at the ready. Ben slowed and brought up his gun. They did the same. They were grinning, sure they had their quarry.

He came up to them and said, "Looks like a standoff, boys. I can take at least three of you, maybe all of you. 'Course, you'd get me, too. I guess that was you, Frenchie, who shot at my girl just now, am I right?"

The Frenchman said, "Damn right, Garçon'. If I can't have 'er, no one else can. I hit her, no?"

"You missed. But now you got me. And that ain't good——fer you."

Just then, the deckhands came around the wall, with Big Harp there in front of them. They slowed to a stop when they saw the rifles. Harp stepped forward, his axe at the ready, a formidable figure. "We' uns 'll handle 'em, Boss!"

"Nope. This man brought himself trouble with that shot at my daughter and now he's goin' to git his payback."

Ben handed Harp his rifle, gave another deckhand his Colt and stripped off his coat and pistol belt, then pulled the big knife from its scabbard at the back of his belt. The blade gleamed in the sunlight and Ben tossed it from hand to hand expertly.

"Come on, Frenchie. This is what you really wanted! Let's see if you're man enough to cross blades with a Mizzouri 'gator!"

The Frenchman was willing. He handed off his rifle, took the pistol from his sash and gave it to one of his group, then pulled out his own knife, a long weapon which had a narrow blade that came to a point in the fashion that later would be called an "Arkansas toothpick." A murderous dagger.

They circled and then the Frenchman leaped forward, his knife hand coming up fast from a low swing that started by his thigh and ended with his wrist being snared by Ben's blocking left hand. At the same instant, Ben slashed with his blade, the razor sharp edge making a cut on the Frenchman's arm right through the leather. He howled and struggled to pull free, then feeling Ben's superior strength, attempted to switch his blade from his right hand.

As he reached across, Ben followed the arm and ran the knife up it once more, the blood running. The man yelled again and tried to kick Ben in the crotch. Ben blocked the leg with his own and took the man to the ground, rolling onto him as the Frenchman tried to bring his legs up and trap Ben's head.

Hunching forward, Ben grinned into the other's face, then reaching down, bit the man's nose, making him squeal like a pig. The Frenchman tried to punch Ben with his bloodied fist, only to feel the other's blade at his throat, edging into his neck, parting the skin, drawing blood.

He gave up then, and lay still as Ben shook his wrist and made the knife in it drop away. Ben, his eyes blazing, spit the end of the man's nose in his face and said, keeping the blade tight on his throat,

"Well, Frenchie. Want yore throat cut—-or should I just carve my initial in you, so that you remember yore manners the next time we come by? Which is it to be, man?" The knife drew more blood as it entered more flesh.

The man mumbled something which Ben took to be the lesser of the two and bringing up his knife, Ben deliberately cut an 'H' on his forehead, two lines running from his hairline to his eyebrows, then connecting them with the bar, the blade going to the bone, making the blood run down the Frenchman's face. The trapper squinted his eyes and gritted his teeth in agony and his body shivered. Ben, watching him, got up slowly from the motionless figure, then reached down and wiped his knife on the man's buckskins. He looked down.

"Next time I see you, Frenchie, I'm goin' to kill you."

He gave the man on the ground a kick. "Hear me, you sonovabitch?" He drew his booted foot back again and the man mumbled, "I hear you."

Ben faced the rest of the trappers, the knife still in his hand. "Any of you want to take up for him?"

He walked close to each of them and they wouldn't look in his eyes as they in turn mumbled their 'no's and shook their heads. He turned away.

"If you'da hit her, Frenchie, yore head would be down by yore feet now. Count yourself lucky you're such a pore shot."

He walked back to the boat surrounded by the deckhands, as the boat whistle blew.

CHAPTER 8.

Fort Buford, Fort Berthold, Bismarck, Fort Pierre, Yankton, Sioux City, and finally Omaha slipped by, with the boat stopping for wood at isolated woodyards and as they got farther south, finally using coal to propel itself down the seemingly endless river. They encountered boats making their way up, the *Helena*, the *Penanah*, the *Josephine*, the *Lucien Lambeau*, and others, Marsh using his whistle to call a greeting as they passed each other. Once it was the *Far West*, captained by Durfee, and the two crafts went to the bank and exchanged some food stuffs and news of the river before going on. Marsh got a box of cigars from his partner and shared them with Ben.

* * *

After the fight at Fort Union, Hite was given a wide berth by the deck passengers and crew, with Big Harp giving a wide smile when he saw Ben on deck. Ben had appreciated the man's backing him—-thought it might have saved his life, in fact, and when he had a chance, drew Harp aside and made him a proposition.

"How much you gittin' fer deck work, Harp?"

"A dollah a day and food, plus whiskey, sah."

"How about $2 a day, less work and better food. Plus better quarters and such."

"What I'se to do, Boss?" Harp was interested in something that would pay twice what he made and he was a little tired of sleeping on the deck.

"You'd be sort of a helper, like, to me."

Harp was dubious. "You pay me $2 a day fer so little as that?"

"Sure. You saw what happened back there at Fort Union—- I need someone to watch my back." He grinned.

Harp laughed, a deep rumble that came up from his chest like a barrel rolling down a gangplank.

"Hah! Hah! Youse din't look lak you needed that much help, Mistah Hite! 'Sides, I tole Capt'n Marsh I'd stay wit' 'im far as St. Louis."

"Well, Harp, let's do this, then. When we reach St. Louis, you come to work fer me. Kin you shoot a rifle an' a pistol?"

The darkie grinned. "Nah, Sah. I jes' use an axe 'er my razor if I needs 'em." From his ragged pants, he pulled out a long straight razor and flipping it, opened it, his hand nearly eclipsing the blade.

"Then, what say I teach you to shoot? I'll want you to pack a pistol which I'll buy fer you when we git to St. Louis. We kin practice off the stern with mine when you git a little time each day." He paused. "That is, if you want the job."

The big man scratched his wooly head. "Guess I does. Where else kin a nigger find 'at kind of day money? But won't the white mens on board say somethin' 'bout you teaching a darkie to shoot a gun?

"Oh, I don't think they'll have much to say."

The whites aboard muttered to themselves or each other, but said nothing to Ben, as he taught Harp to shoot the Henry and his pistol off the fantail of the boat each morning.

* * *

58

Two weeks, later, just before St. Louis, Ben found a time when Captain Marsh could talk and stated that he wanted to employ Big Harp. Marsh was curious and Ben told him that he wanted the big man as a sort of servant and bodyguard.

The captain laughed. "From what I've seen of you, Mr. Hite, that would be a good idea! Sure, take him if you want. All I ask is that you give him enough to git on back to the river here if you let him go."

"That's fair, Captain. I kin promise that."

* * *

They gathered Harp up when they disembarked at St. Louis's busy levy, leaving the other hands to stare as they began to unload without him. Katy was astounded at the many boats tied up along the miles long levy there. Her count trailed off at fifty but there were more. The cab service was fairly organized along the shore and they were able, with Harp's piercing whistle, to secure one whose obliging driver helped Harp load the baggage in the rear of the vehicle. "Take us to the best hotel, please." Ben instructed.

"That'd be the Stockdale. She's mighty pricey, though, Sir."

"We'll splurge a little. Go ahead."
"Yes, Sir."

As they got out of the taxi, the doorman, a huge uniformed Irishman, came over to them and said, "This 'ere establishment ain't got no rooms fer niggers. Sorry. House rule."

"Listen, Mick, I just hired this man off the boat and I want him cleaned up and dressed right. He's goin' to work fer me. Kin you help us out with that?"

The doorman looked at Harp and said, "I guess so. It'll cost yer. He's about my size and I could sell you some o' my auld stuff." He looked down at Harp's huge bare feet and said, "Don't know about gittin' him shod, though.

Guess the cobbler could make him up some boots by tomorry." Ben took out a bill and handed to him. The Irishman smiled. This could relieve his boredom <u>and</u> pay handsomely.

"Is there some place close by that he could be put up, then? I mean a clean place that he could have a bath and a good bed while you git him squared away."

"All right, sir. I'll take care of it." He let out a piercing whistle that made Harp grin. It was a twin to the one he could produce, himself. Bellboys came on the run and gathered up their luggage, taking it into the plush establishment. The doorman took Harp in tow and the two disappeared around the corner.

* * *

It was a new Harp whom the Doorman, Mr. Phikes, presented to Ben and Katy the next day. He had bathed, his hair was cut, his old rags thrown away and he was wearing presentable clothes, with gleaming new boots on his feet. He had a valise, which Phikes said, had three changes inside. Phikes presented his bill and Ben paid it, along with some money for his board and lodging. Then he tipped a gold eagle, which made Phikes smile again.

Ben took Harp in hand then, and the two went to the gun store and bought him a Colt .45, a twin to the one Ben carried. This, and the Elgin watch and gold fob Ben fastened to his vest made Harp grin like an opened piano. 'Big Harp, ready to strut his stuff!'

"An' I still gots my razor, Sah." He pulled it from his back pocket.

"Keep it handy, Harp. Like I do mine." Ben smiled as he pulled his knife from behind his back and showed it to the darkie, whose grin got even wider.

* * *

60

Three days later, Ben had gotten his fill of St. Louis. He had, with Katy on his arm, talked to three separate doctors about their medical educations. Armed now with information as to how they might fulfill Katy's dream of becoming a doctor, Ben had elected to go on to New York, which meant taking the trains.

The Illinois Central ran through to Chicago, where they laid over a day to make their connections on the Wabash and Toledo, then into Toledo, Ohio, up to Detroit, Michigan, and finally, on the fourth day, to Buffalo, New York.

* * *

By now, all were heartily sick of riding, with the smelly, dirty coal smoke eddying back into the compartments and the constant hawkers of food, drink and curios yelling, going up and down the aisles, along with screaming children and smoking men. But, the New York Central railroad, which connected Buffalo to New York City, was a pleasant surprise. It was clean and the coal smoke was diverted by an extra tall smoke stack diverter on the engine. The conductors didn't allow hawkers for most of the journey, limiting them to five minutes at each stop as to their time aboard. And the train was also sectioned off into family cars and adults only cars, which afforded the trio some relief from the noise of the other passengers.

The last item was an added relief: smoking only in designated cars. Ben liked a cigar or a chew as well as any, but he sympathized with Katy's repugnance to the perpetual smoke, and so he had limited himself in that regard. Harp was a chewer and a swallower. In his large jaws, a wad of tobacco didn't show, anyway and he could nurse a cud along for an hour or more.

Time passed quickly and through the scrubbed windows, the passengers delighted in seeing the pastoral countryside change into urban sprawl before reaching the city. Coming into Grand Central Depot, as it was called, the train jolted to a stop and let off steam. The Station served two other railways besides the New York Central and the place was somewhat crowded. However, working their way through the press of people was easy, as Harp bulled his way and they followed. Outside, cabs were lined up and Harp used his whistle to catch a driver's attention.

He and Harp retrieved the luggage from the baggage car as Ben and Katy waited, then, after finding out they wanted to go to Queens Borough, the cabby recommended the Wolcott Hotel as a premium lodging close to the Women's Medical College and hospital that Doctor Clemence Lozier and Elizabeth Blackwell had established on the corner of 2nd Avenue and 12th street. He took them there and they checked in. The driver got a handsome tip.

The Wolcott was progressive in its handling of customers accompanied by servants, and had accommodations for them on two floors, which consisted of small chambers within the suites which had separate beds and other conveniences. The floors had men's and women's bathrooms for the servants use. The suites themselves had luxurious bathrooms and a separate lounge. Ben noted all this with satisfaction, and decided to return to the lobby and take the suite for a week, which he did.

He paid Harp up to then and tried to give him the next day off. Harp balked at this.

"Aren't I s'posed to pertect you, Sah? This' ere's a strange, big town and no tellin' what might be lurkin' 'round a corner! 'Sides, I got no place to go, anyway, 'round 'ere. It's all white folks."

"Well...All right. We're just goin' to this college place and see if Katy kin enroll. Guess you might just follow along with us."

Harp grinned, "Yassuh. That be what I do! Watch yer back."

* * *

The next day, followed by Harp, they went out onto the street and with Katy taking her father's arm, walked the three blocks to the college entrance. Even in New York, people turned as stared as the trio went by. Katy shivered as they went inside, and Ben was astute enough to realize that she was apprehensive about her future and how this featureless building might figure into it. The Territory was far away and both were conscious of the strangeness of the city.

Inside, the receptionist received them courteously and after inquiring as to the nature of their visit, asked them to be seated. They sat in pews by the wall close to the entrance and Ben noticed the odd smell, which reminded him of the hospitals he'd been inside during the war. Medicinal odors mixed with that of stringent formaldehyde and alcohol permeated the air. It brought back unpleasant memories, ones he had pushed into a room in his mind and shut the door on and not for the first time, he wished that Katy might have chosen some other field to take up. Looking at her, though, he realized that she was eager, excited and inquisitive. She seemed to breathe the air in as one might inhale a perfume.

Then a woman approached them—-a matronly starched figure, her hair covered like a nun, who exuded authority and purpose. She held out her hand as she came up and Ben took it automatically..

"Hello, I'm Doctor Lozier. You wanted to see me?"

"Doctor, I'm Ben Hite. This is Katy—Katherine Hite Barnes, my step-daughter. And Big Harp, our... man." Harp grinned and ducked his head. She nodded, amused. Ben explained,

63

"Katy wants to be a doctor. I...want what she wants, I guess you could say. I'll foot the bill."

The woman turned to Katy and grasping her hands, turned the palms up. "Well, she isn't a stranger to work, I see. Good hands. But what about your mind, dear? Could you pass the courses of instruction? Our work is mental as well as physical."

"I can work, Doctor. I <u>will</u> work, do whatever you tell me, and I have never had any trouble with studies, but I know I am probably behind in some. I'd work real hard to catch up."

The doctor noticed her determination and it struck her favorably.

"Come in, then, to my office and we will get acquainted."

* * *

After an exhausting hour of questions, Doctor Lozier finally came out with,

"Well, she is behind in nearly every subject, but... I like her spirit and her grit. And her mind is quick. Yes. I will take her on. But, becoming a doctor isn't something to be accomplished overnight. It will take three years, likely longer. Are you prepared to make that commitment, Katy?"

"Oh, yes, Ma'am!" She was, Ben saw, radiant at the woman's acceptance. Clearly, she had doubted she'd be accepted.

"And, Mr. Hite, it will cost money—her tuition and her food will be paid by her work in the hospital. But she'll require a clothing allowance, rooming and other funds for miscellaneous expenses such as books and uniforms. Can you supply that, Sir?"

Ben grinned. "I planned to do that, Doctor. How much a year?"

"At least $500."

"Then let's say a thousand a year. Three years. Do I write the check to the college?"

She smiled. "That would be fine. Very fine! And helpful, Sir." Clearly, she had been somewhat dubious as to whether he could pay it. Ben's clothing was provincial and his manner likewise. She was relieved and her eyes got a little wider when she saw he had made the check out for $4000.00. She looked up and he said,

"The extra thousand is a donation to the school from a woman named Siccoolum. I heard that you could maybe use the money." The name made Katy's eyes glisten.

Ben had talked to a doctor he had heard of from the war who was practicing in St. Louis. That gentleman had known all about Elizabeth Blackwell's and Doctor Lozier's struggle to provide an institution for young women to follow the medical profession. He'd said it was slowly gaining recognition but was facing an uphill battle against prejudice and downright ignorance, one myth being that women weren't smart as men and couldn't master the subject matter. The doctor was sympathetic himself, and Ben, remembering Siccoolum, had decided to give the donation in her memory.

"If Katy needs more, I will put some money into an account for her at a bank here. Could you suggest one?"

"Certainly. I use the Commerce Bank just down the street here. A sound one, I believe. And one sympathetic to our endeavors."

"Then we'll do our business there." He stood up. "When might you want her to come?"

"You have just arrived in New York?"

"Yes, Ma'am, we have."

"Then, I would suggest you take in some concerts and perhaps the theater. One of Shakespeare's best, *Hamlet*, is being put on at the Opera House. You might like to take it in before you leave the city. I assume you will be returning to your holdings out west?"

Ben grinned. "Well, Ma'am, maybe Katy will come to enjoy such things, but I think that I will have to pass on them. My interests are more to going to a riverboat show, or maybe a good gun store. Honey, let's go down to the bank so that we can open the account for you. Then, maybe tomorrow, if the Doctor will tell you what you need for clothes, we kin go out and buy them. Then you could come back here the next day and get settled in."

* * *

The bank had a staid, stodgy look about it, and the manager was likewise, a Mr. Custis, who helped them get an account set up and took the $10,000 deposit without raising an eyebrow in surprise. Katy, though, said, "Father! It's too much! I'll never use it all!"

"Listen, Honey, You know how far away I'll be. If you need money, it'd take weeks for me to get it to you. This way, if you need it, just come down here and git it. And sometime, if I might be short and need some funds, some of it'll maybe be here. We'll put some in savings, an' some in a checking account fer you."

CHAPTER 9.

Leaving Katy in New York was as hard on Ben as it was on her. Harp saw it and did what he could to raise his boss out of the depression he was feeling. Despite himself, he was coming to have some feelings of affection for the white man. It wasn't until they reached Detroit and they were walking through the train station that Ben was jolted out of his funk. He was jostled by a man who excused himself and walked on. Ben, a little streetwise, felt for his wallet in his coat. It was gone. He whirled and Harp, beside him, knew immediately what had happened and took off after the disappearing figure.

For a big man, he was quick on those immense feet and catching the man, he grabbed him by the collar and yanked him down. Ben, though, had watched for and seen the second act, which was that the man had handed off the wallet to an accomplice, another who turned innocently and started to leave the facility. Ben ran and tackled him, yelling, 'Thief, Thief!"

The man tried to fight and Ben slid his knife out and said, "The wallet, man, 'er I'll slit yer throat!"

The other carefully brought the wallet out and handed it over. Ben took it and riffled through the bills. He had two thousand dollars in it and it seemed all there. Bystanders were gathering and then a policeman bustled through the mob, "''Ere now, 'Er now, wot's this?" When he saw Ben with his knife still out, he pulled his gun.

"Drop the knife!"

Ben did. The officer had a no-nonsense look that spoke of experience and competence.

About that time, Harp came up with the other man and Ben explained himself. The policemen, for another older one had arrived, took one look at the man that Harp had collared and gathered them both up.

"Ye caught a couple good ones there, Sir! "Fast" Johnny Lark and Oscar "The Dipper" Harper. Both pickpockets and purse snatchers with long records! This'll put 'em back inta the pen, I'd bet."

Ben had to go down to the station and sign the complaint, then they were able to go on their way. Luckily, their train was an evening one and they didn't miss it, but the excitement and getting his wallet back intact brought Ben out of his dark mood. He treated Harp to a couple drinks and cigars in the bar car. The Negro conductor, passing through, took a second look at the big darkie sitting there, enjoying a drink with the white man. That was something he couldn't remember having seen before. It wasn't supposed to occur, as according to the train rules Negroes were excluded from the bar, but seeing the bulk of the two men, he wisely let it go. Like other negroes, he was used to prejudice, but that didn't mean he had to like it, or abet it.

* * *

From Toledo, they took the Wabash again, which got them back to Chicago, then the Illinois Central, which carried them on down to St. Louis. There, Ben checked in again at the Stockdale and they greeted Phikes, the doorman at his post, standing there in the rain. He took Harp off to the lodging house and Ben took his leisure in his room after a hot bath and clean clothes, a little lonely now with Katy absent. His thoughts turned to the children of the Perkins train.

68

From the letters Miles had writtten and their replies, he had gotten some information about the pitiful few survivors of the train massacre. There had been seventeen young children. They had all been under the age of six at the time of the slaughter and had later been rescued from the Mormons and Indians by Doctor Forney, the Indian Agent for the Paiutes. In a report to the federal government, he had written that the children had been kept in a deplorable condition and had taken much care and attention after he had retrieved them.

Sixteen had eventually been returned to their relatives in Boone and Johnson County, Arkansas, in the northwestern corner of the state. From what Miles could learn, they had been survivors of the Dunlap, Miller, Huff, Tackitt, Baker and Fancher families, most from the town of Harrison. There was also perhaps a young boy, Thomas Tackitt, who was said to have been traded by the Paiutes to the Navajos. He'd not been recovered and Ben had wondered about the youngster's fate.

Harrison, in Boone County, was not far from Taney County, where he had grown up, in the Ozarks about thirty miles away, on Crooked Creek. He weighed the options of stopping at home for a visit. He would like to see his mother, if she were still alive, but it would likely provoke a family fight. Thinking about it kept him awake part of the night.

The next day, with Harp at his heels, he bought tickets on the Missouri and Arkansas Railroad and they rode it down to Springfield, the end of the rails. From there, they would have to go by horses. Ben found a reputable livery and rented a light carriage and a team of decent horses for the trip, which would be close to a hundred miles one way yet, to Harrison. He had decided to stop at his homesite and chance the trouble it would cause, to see his mother once more. They loaded some food, blankets and camp gear in the conveyance and were off.

* * *

Camping out at night, Ben got to know Harp and he, his boss. Ben, with his years of experience during the war and after in the mountains, had plenty of skill at making them comfortable out away from towns. Harp, on the other hand, was a street-wise city man, and it seemed a reversal of roles for awhile, and a routine was established.

Harp collected wood and set up the canvas shelter Ben had brought along, making their beds. Ben, meanwhile, made the fire and did the cooking. Harp cleaned up afterward. In the morning, Harp brought the horses in and grained them while Ben made coffee and some breakfast, then they hitched up and resumed their journey. Harp liked to talk and his stories of the river were interesting. He also liked to sing, and knew many songs. Ben liked to listen to the deep bass voice and sometimes joined in, when he knew one. They got along well and the miles sped by.

* * *

Going back home was like walking in a swamp in hip deep mud and water at night. The journey in some ways was a trying one to Ben. He dreaded what he'd find back there. Hite Hollow lay in the foothills of the Ozarks deep in the woods. South out of Joplin and almost on the Arkansas line, Ben and Harp followed the winding dirt path through the overhanging trees and finally came to a clearing in which there was a tumble down cabin, a sagging barn and some outbuildings, including a stable. Once, Ben remembered, the place had looked prosperous. Now, it looked rundown and forlorn.

He stopped the carriage in the overgrown yard and surveyed the house. On the porch, rose a man, who came out from the shadow and looked at Ben. He was familiar and Ben said, "Linc! Is that you?"

"Howdy there, Ben. Come home at last, huh?"

Now, Ben saw that his younger brother had his left arm missing just above the elbow. He got down from the carriage and strode forward, still unsure of his welcome. The other man approached him with a limp, though, and threw his right arm about him, hugging him. Then, he raised his voice.

"Liz! Come here and see! It's Ben!"

From inside the house, a lean woman came to the door and stood there, looking. She didn't speak.

Linc turned back to Ben and said,

"She kain't talk. Jayhawkers cut her tongue off. Wouldn't tell where we was holed up. Shot her, too, but she lived. Surprised us all."

"Sorry to hear that, Linc. Any kids?"

Lincoln Hite looked about. He was a younger, smaller, leaner version of Ben, black haired, with deepset eyes that bored into one and a tentative smile that showed a front tooth missing.

"Oh yeah. Half a dozen. They're all hidin' out. Scared of strangers." He yelled, "This here's yer Uncle! Ben! The one who fit fer the Union!"

He turned then, and looking at Harp, said,

"Who'se the nigger? Big ole' boy, ain't he?"

Ben said shortly, "Harp's his own man. He works fer me." Ben tried to steer the conversation away from what could be sensitive ground. "So, how's the rest of the family?"

Linc spit green tobacco juice. "What fambly? Ma's dead. Pa's dead. Kilt by Union cavalry over by Springfield. Matt, Hi and John are all dead, too. Fact is," He hitched his pants which were tied up by twine. "You and me is all there is left, brother."

"Linc. I'm sorry to hear it." The news hit him hard, though he had steeled himself for it. The other shrugged.

71

"Jest the way it is, Ben. Only one buried here is Ma. Died of the flux——that and heartbreak, I guess. Always wondered if you mighta made it, she did. Now we know. She be buried over by the big oak there." He spit again, then offered Ben a chew. He obligingly bit off a hunk and returned the twist.

From around the house and by the barn, Ben could see faces peeking out at them, one, braver than the rest, was coming toward them, a little boy of about five. He was black haired like his father, with Hite features: the slash of a mouth, the square chin and deep set eyes, the blocky shoulders.

He marched up to them and said, "I'm Montgomery. Dad calls me Monte. Pleased ta meet 'cha." He held out a grubby hand. Ben gravely shook it. Then, from their hiding places, the other kids came creeping out and soon surrounded them, to Ben's secret delight. There were three boys and three girls, the girls older and the boys younger. They were lean, dirty wood rats——typical Hites, Ben thought.

* * *

Ben made camp up by the clear spring that fed the run and provided the house and barn with clear water. Linc apologized for the lack of room in the house, but Ben said they were used to sleeping out and it was no problem. After they had eaten the possum Linc had killed that day, the family came up and gathered at their fire and Ben saw that the woman walked with a decided limp, too, and had a shoulder that was lower than the rest of her body. Linc saw him glance at her and said,

"Shot her up some, 'afore they taken off."

Her eyes burned at him and he saw a residual hatred of anything Yankee in her demeanor, though mute and silent. He couldn't blame her.

The children all were curious about Harp and when he finally broke his silence, some of them almost ran at his deep voice. He laughed then and they soon were reassured. He liked children and knew how to entertain them, taking out his harmonica and playing and singing. Even the woman caught the music and her feet began tapping. From the folds of her dress, she produced a little flute and expertly began accompanying Harp. The evening ended late, the children protesting having to go to bed. She went along down with them and Ben said,

"The place here yours now, Linc?"

Linc gazed fixedly into the fire. "Unless you claim it, by right of being older, Ben."

"Nope. I don't want it, just wanted to make sure you owned it. How do you live? Don't see any mules around or ground broke fer crops."

"No mules 'cause there ain't no money. Nope. Jest a little huntin' an' fishing, is all. Trap some in the winter. The fur critters is near all gone, though. No deer left, neither."

"I got some money, Linc. Let's go tomorrow and git you some mules and some equipment." Ben stirred the fire and Harp threw another log on.

"You'd do that fer us?"

"Sure. You're family, Linc. All there is left."

"That's so, ain't it?" Linc whispered. He spit in the fire and then got up to go. "Glad you lived to come back home, Ben."

* * *

The next day, after Ben had visited the family's graveyard under the spreading big oak, they went into the little village of Taney Crossing and directed by Linc, found a man who had a good pair of mules for sale. He threw in the harness and sold them a steel plow and harrow, too. Ben paid cash and the farmer promised to

73

deliver the plow and harrow in his freight wagon that afternoon. He would also bring the headstone that Ben had ordered from the stone mason.

Seed was harder to come by and it took a trip back to Joplin to purchase it. While there, Ben stocked up on flour, salt, sugar, coffee, beans and the other necessities of life that he knew Linc's family was lacking. The purchases filled the carriage and Ben and Harp, too, both enjoyed seeing the life come back into the faces of the parents as they watched the kids gobble candy Ben had brought them and helped unload the carriage of the food and clothing. Ben had tried to think of everything and a tear squeezed from Liz's eyes at the bountiful surplus they were given.

Linc had taken the mules and with the plow delivered, had already turned nearly an acre of the good bottom ground. He wanted Ben to come see how well the mules had done, and when Ben walked down to the plowed ground, took the occasion, with tears in his eyes, to thank him wholeheartedly. Then the two men, working together, erected the headstone over their mother's grave.

* * *

Two days later, Ben, after promising to stop on the way back, hitched up and they headed on down to Harrison, thirty miles away. The town was thriving, with lead and zinc mines and a smelter there to provide employment. Union soldiers had founded the place after the war and it was a pleasant place, set in the midst of cotton and fruit tree farms. They put up at the Park Hotel, a large two story frame structure with a good restaurant. Harp, though, had to eat in the kitchen, which didn't faze him, as his meal was likely better than Ben's.

Once situated, Ben set off to the newspaper office to gather some information. With the gossipy editor, Mr. Fairwell, Ben soon was able to find the trail of the whereabouts of the orphan children. Their folks had been of Methodist and Presbyterian religion and he directed Ben to the ministers, who knew exactly what Ben needed to know. The children had been taken in by their grandfolks, mainly. They wondered about his concern and Ben knew they suspected a Mormon connection. He liked the looks of both the men and took them into his confidence.

After having an opportunity to meet most of the children, who now were older and to a person, withdrawn and quiet, the one little girl missing an arm that had been shot off, he went with the ministers to the bank there and opened accounts for each of the kids, putting in equal amounts of the $100,000 he had gotten from the Mormon leader, $5,682.35, including the seventeenth share, which he explained, would go to the young boy still kept by the Navajos, if he should be found and brought home to Harrison. The ministers would oversee the money for them.

Both churches held a celebration and pot luck in the children's and his honor, and he got to meet most of the community. Word of what he had done spread and some of the newspapers of the state carried the article. That brought in more money in the form of donations, which pleased the community and Ben. He was satisfied that the money had done some good.

* * *

Back at Hite Hollow a few days later, he was startled to see the changed aspect of the place. Linc had hired a couple men and they had started to put the buildings and the house in order. The field was plowed and planted. Linc had even brought down water from the spring and piped it indoors for his wife. She greeted him with an unreserved smile, the hatred gone from her eyes, and this time the two men were swarmed by the children, who asked for candy. Ben delighted in obliging them with their own sacks and they whooped and jigged about the yard as the grown-ups tried to talk.

He went with Linc the next day and they surveyed a farm which adjoined his on the north. The upshot was that Ben bought the half section piece, handing the deed over to his astounded brother. That purchase, with the money he left with him, bode fair to the future prosperity of the family, which meant so much to Ben.

"One more thing, Linc. I see you haven't got a good watch. Here's one to remember me by." He took the solid gold Jurgensen from his pocket, unhooked the fob and chain and put it in his hands.

"Keeps good time, Linc. You being on yore way to bein' a successful farmer, you need a good watch."

* * *

They left a few days later, with the family waving a sad goodbye. Monte swore he was coming to visit Ben just as soon as he got old enough. Ben invited them all and the sincerity of his invitation made a lasting impression on them.

CHAPTER 10.

Back at St. Louis once more, Ben paid Harp his wages and asked him if he was ready to quit. He'd done what he'd set out to do: get Katy settled, find the survivors of the massacre and give the money to them, and see how his own family was doing and if he could help them. Now, he was going back to the mountains and Harp was welcome to come if he wanted, at the day wage he'd been getting.

"The work might be harder, though, Harp. Skinning buffalo, fighting Indians, and such." Ben grinned. The two had gotten to be friends.

Harp laughed. "I'se ready! When we go?"

"We'll see what boats are headin' to Benton. I need to get a new watch and we need to buy you a rifle."

They walked down to Shugart's, a jewelry store close by the hotel and Ben picked out one of their finest, a solid gold J.W. Benson English repeater with an accompanying heavy chain and fob. The fob had some nuggets and a little gold buffalo on it, which Ben thought might be an omen. He and Harp then walked off down the street toward the gun shop.

At Finstead's, Ben bought Harp a Sharps .45/90 rifle and a .44 Winchester. They also picked up shells for all their weapons, since they were so much cheaper there. The one-eyed clerk said that he'd see they got on the right boat if Ben would send word as to which one they were taking upriver.

That done, they walked along the waterfront and decided on trying to get passage on a new boat they saw, the *Anson LaFarge*, which Ben thought would have little trouble getting up the Missouri. The shallow drafted craft was the epitome of what an upper riverboat should be: shallow hulled, drawing perhaps two feet, a snag room, stern wheeled, with a donkey engine fore and aft, and with heavy planked railings waist high to take any bullets that might come her way from the shore. A man was guarding it from his seat on the stern and Harp called out to him,

"Hey there, Spike! How's chances fer gitting passage on this old scow?"

Spike called back,

"Hello Harp! Sure, we got room yet, I think. The Cap'n'll be back pretty soon, but the purser's in his cabin. I'll go git 'im. Guard the gangplank fer me."

He went off and soon came back with an elderly man whose glasses made his eyes look like an owl's. He stood by the gangplank.

"Yes, Sir. What kin I do fer ye?"

Ben said, "Do you have any cabins available for Benton?"

"That we do. Four left. At $175 for a single. That includes yer place at the table."

"Any cabins with two bunks?"

"Yes, Sir. At $250 the cabin, with both passengers food. But I doubt the bunks would fit Big Harp there, if that's yer idea."

Harp said, "Ah don't mind the deck, Sah. If I sleeps in a cabin, the hands'll think I got a case of the uppities."

Ben looked at him and replied, "Well, You're my responsibility, Harp. We'll take a single cabin and fix up a bed on the floor fer you."

He turned and spoke to the purser. "We'll take a double at the $250 but lay down a bunk fer Harp on the deck. We kin use the upper bunk fer stowage. That all right?"

"I s'pose we could do that." the Purser, John Sykes, said. "Ben Hite, is that right?"

Ben was surprised. Though he knew some of the steamboat people, this purser was not one. "Yes, that's right."

The older man nodded. "Thought it was you. Seen you on the Benton wharf a few times. You were pointed out to me and Captain Harvey as being Lakey Steele's partner in the freightin' business. I've done freight consignments with Steele many times. Heard you had hired Harp there off Marsh's boat."

He came over the plank and shook hands with Ben, then, hesitating a little, with Harp. "How are you, Harp? Wantin' a deck job?"

"Nah, Sah. Workin' for Mr. Hite here now."

"Maybe better, anyway. The crew is Irish and you know how they kin be. Micks and niggers don't mix too well. Well, why don't you come aboard in the morning and you and Spike there can fix up a bed fer you in cabin #3. It's a little bigger and you should be able to stretch out in it."

The racial aspersions were used by most people of that time and Harp took no offense, being used to it on the river, even using them himself.

"Thank you, Sah. I will."

Ben paid over the money to retain the cabin and they started to leave the wharf to return to the hotel, just as a young man came strolling up. Sykes introduced them to Harvey Allen, his captain. Introductions were made by Sykes and Ben sized the captain up. He was a stocky young man who walked with a little limp to his gait and had an air of authority about him. He packed a Colt revolver in a holster around his middle and Ben, an observer of such things, detected another pistol in his vest pocket. Clearly, the captain was ready for trouble if it came. Ben liked his open countenance, his courteous aspect and straight forward manner. They'd get along. The next morning, the *Anson Lafarge* slipped her moorings and headed upstream to enter the mouth of the Missouri for her three thousand miles journey.

CHAPTER 11.

The trip up the Missouri on the *Anson Lafarge* was fast and effortless. Her shallow draft, strong engines and competent Irish crew complemented the expertise of the captain, who also served as her pilot, a job he obviously loved, though he was breaking in a new cub pilot, a young Irishman named Jake Cable. The boat, he told Ben, could carry 250 tons of freight, more if they were running on coal rather than the bulky wood, and had deck room, sixty cabin passengers and 100 or so deck passengers.

They were moored at Yankton, waiting for the crew to finish unloading freight for the wagon yard there and Allen had invited Ben up to the wheel house for a cup of coffee. The young cub was working diligently in his journal, drawing in the last few miles of the river, with their bars, snags, rocks and other hazards. The depths of the river were also penciled in and Allen, observing him, said that he should remember also to include the time of day, as the water level dropped or raised some according to when it was. Ben was interested to see the boy's intensity and when he left to get them more coffee, asked Allen about his cub.

"He's the young brother of a man I knew in St. Louis, a friend who was killed in the war. His family is destitute and I took him on for their sake. I think he's going to make a pilot, though, with time. He works hard at it, like I did when I was his age, under a man this boat is named after. A hell of a riverman."

He turned and spit in the stained cuspidor by the wheel and the old dog there lifted his head, then laid it back down. Allen looked at it thoughtfully, thinking about whether to tell this new acquaintance the dog's story. He decided not to. They were new friends but he still to this day, had some qualms about the truth of the matter.

The dog had been with him ever since Joe Cable had died, during the War, and sometimes Harvey thought that maybe the dog <u>was</u> Joe, come back to life. And that was silly——preposterous. Hite would laugh at him. In fact, he'd not told anyone his suspicions. Probably wouldn't. They'd think he was nuts and that was not the image a boat captain wanted to put out to the paying public. Captains were supposed to be solid, full of common sense, reliable, not somebody who believed that a mongrel dog was a reincarnated friend. He pushed the thought out of his mind for the thousandth time.

"And you were saying, Ben, that your son, Fred, is partnered now with Steele in the freight business out of Benton to the mines? 'Course, I know Steele."

"That's right."

Ben spit in the direction of the cuspidor and made it ring. He didn't ordinarily chew too much but enjoyed it once in awhile. Allen, though, was addicted and chewed it steadily, even when he was drinking coffee. The only time it was absent from his mouth was when he was eating or sleeping. It was a common habit and most of the men of the day indulged, though some opted for a pipe or a cigar if they could get one. Ben preferred a cigar, really. He looked at the old dog laying in the sun.

"He's not really my son by blood, but my adopted boy. I was placer mining over in the Tobacco Roots by Sheridan the winter of '66 and this dog came scratchin' at my door...."

He told Harvey the story of the blizzard.

"He came scratching on the door of my cabin and got me to follow him to where these kids was, just about froze to death under a tree and...."

* * *

The telling was finished just about the time that the unloading was and Allen, from his seat at the bench there, said,

"That's quite a story, Ben. I bet you'll be glad to see those youngsters again when you get home. Just now, though, I better get this boat to goin' or we'll be held up here tonight. We need to make a few more miles before dark."

He pressed the whistle pedal and a deep toned wail came from the instrument perched high on the top of the escapement valve pipe. Ben, knowing passengers were not allowed in the wheel house while the boat was underway, took the empty cups and headed down the gangway to his cabin.

* * *

Far to the north and west of Yankton, in that area which later would be known as the "Big Dry" between the Missouri River and the Yellowstone, smoke was rising, the smell making the buffalo and antelope scatter from its vicinity. Two men sat their horses and looked down at the blackened wagons and the scattered remnants of their hunting outfit.

"Wonder where Charlie got off to?" Will ventured. They'd walked their horses close to the fire, which was dying down, a few hides and the wagon tongues still showing flames.

Charlie Nelson was their skinner and cook. His body wasn't, as far as they could tell, in the fire. Hank watched a magpie light on a sagebrush a hundred yards away and walked his horse over there.

"Here he is...but you don't want to see him." Will spurred his horse to where Hank was and gagged as he looked down at the mutilated body. "Christ! Why do they have to do that to a man? Why can't they just shoot him and be done with it?"

"I guess they just don't care much fer whites killin' off their meat supply."

Hank swung down wearily and taking his knife out, started digging a grave. Will went back and looked around the devastated camp for the shovel but it was gone, maybe deep in the embers. He went back, and pulling his own knife, started on the other end of the marked out grave. Hours later, they piled the last of the rocks on the top of the site and Hank stuck the carved piece of half burned board at its head, placing more rocks to hold it upright.

> *Charlie Nelson*
> *killed by Indians*
> *Sept. 1878*
> *R.I.P.*

Will had written a poem on another board with a bullet point and stuck it under a rock on the grave.

> *Charlie Nelson, our cook, died today*
> *Take him up, please, Oh Lord, we pray.*
> *It was Indians who made him pass,*
> *No more beans, no more gas.*

"Hate to leave those dead buffs to rot but can't do much else, with our wagons burned and our stock run off." Hank looked to the south, then to the north. "I make it about a hundred miles south to the Yellowstone, a hundred north to the Missouri. But that seems to be the way those Indians were traveling. What you want to do?"

Will Kernzy drew a blackened hand over his brow, deepening the charcoal smear there. "Hellsfire, I don't know. What's south there...Coulson's Landing?"

"Yeah. I don't know fer sure what that is. A boat stop fer hides, I guess, if any make it up that far."

"You got any money?"

"Nope. It was all in my gear. You?"

Will fished in his vest pocket and pulled out two 20 dollar gold pieces. He flipped one to Hank, who caught it. "Guess we both got enough fer a bottle 'er two and some meals. Let's head on back to Benton."

They turned their horses and headed north. They had no food, water bags half full, weary horses and little ammo left, so they traveled cautiously, walking part of the time, careful not to skyline themselves. The miles passed silently, and with Will's bad knee, agonizingly.

In late afternoon, Hank ventured, "That last sentence of yer poem—didn't think it was a bit irreverent?"

Will pondered for a mile or more, never given to a quick answer. "Well, it was all I could come up with on short notice, but maybe *"No one to weep—no son, no lass,"* might have been a little more appropriate. Don't think I'll go back and change it now, though."

They crossed the Nez Perce trail as the tribe fled north some miles farther on.

CHAPTER 12.

Fort Benton

"Papers all say the Army's havin' a hell of a time catchin' up to the Nez Perce. They're tryin' to make it on up to Canada, sounds like. Chief Joseph and his warriors fought Gibbon to a standstill on the Big Hole an' they lost 'em." Harvey Allen commented over coffee at the Grand cafe to a table full of his ex-passengers, which included Ben. They had just finished a prodigious breakfast and were enjoying their smokes and coffee after a late night in the bar.

"Wouldn't have hurt a damn thing if they'd just let 'em go on north," Ben said. "They just want to be left alone. And then it would be Canada's problem."

"Well, I heered they killed some people and stole some horses where they was, over on the Snake River. Only good Injun is a dead one, far as I'm concerned!" Another man interjected, with a jarring laugh.

Ben looked at him thoughtfully. The man was an easterner who'd come up to join his relations at Virginia City. He'd had been full of contradictory comments the whole trip up the river, and last night at the bar had nearly been called out by one of the other men, who had gotten tired of his know-it-all tirades. Allen had separated them and calmed them down, but privately, Ben thought that the loudmouth likely would not last too long on the frontier. Men of his ilk were short-timers.

The comment struck Harvey Allen wrong, too, Ben saw. Both looked at each other and shook their heads slightly. Both left the table and settled their bill. Stepping outside, Ben offered Allen a fresh cigar. Lighting up, their gaze drifted to the street as two men rode by, their horses drooping as much as the two in the saddles. Ben's eyes lighted with recognition and he called, "Hey! Hank! Will!"

At the hail, the heads of both men turned and they reined back to the front of the hotel where Ben and Allen stood. Ben shook his head at the sight of them.

"You boys look like you bin in the war——all over again." He said with a grin. Both men's eyes followed his hand as he took another puff on the long cheroot. He correctly interpreted their stare for what it was, having seen it many times in the past.

He gestured, "C'mon. Git on down and come in. I'll see yer horses git to the livery."

As the men dismounted with difficulty, Ben introduced them to Allen and the three shook hands. Then Ben said, "Looks like a feed, some drinks, then a bath might be in order."

Will croaked, "Drinks first, then food, then the bath." Hank echoed his friend's wish and they went in to the hotel. Allen bid them 'Goodbye' as he had to rejoin his boat and make ready to head back down-river.

* * *

Some whiskies and some large steaks made them feel like they were among the living again. While they ate, Ben told them of his travels back east, giving them the short version, for he could see they were exhausted. He had gotten them a room with some difficulty, as the hotel was nearly full to overflowing. Now he made sure they navigated the stairs and that they had their baths ready for them, then went back down to the bar, where to his dismay, the loudmouth passenger, Victor Prentice, was harping away to a group of half-drunks on the Nez Perce situation as he saw it. The dimwit grated on Ben and he turned around and headed back up the stairs to his room and settled in for the night. Harp was there already, and the two talked awhile, then as the hotel gradually quieted, took to their beds.

The next morning, Ben waited for hours in the cafe, hoping the two men might make it up and down to eat. Finally, about eleven, Hank and Will made their appearance and Ben ordered them a huge breakfast. Watching the two take in their food, he could tell they were half-starved and it was long before their attention came off their plates. Finally, though, they were ready for coffee and Ben asked,

"So tell me what happened. Thought you were out of the hide business and into steamboats."

Hank lit cigars for Will and himself and replied,

"The *Elena* snagged and went down just outa Pierre. Lost the whole cargo and a couple passengers who was drunk an' couldn't swim. Insurance didn't cover it all and us investors got stuck with a big loss. Took ever'thing we had to meet our end, so we went on back to huntin'." He blew smoke and slurped some coffee, then continued.

"We headed southeast over to the head of the Porcupine and Will and me were about to make a good stand, when we got jumped by a bunch of young bucks. If Will's horse hadn't snorted and got our attention, they'da put us under. As it was, it was a damn close thing. We forted up on a little hill where we was shootin' and made it tough fer 'em. Killed two apiece when they thought they was goin' to run over us, then out-shot 'em long range an' killed a couple more." He blew smoke, reliving the episode.

"They had Sharps rifles themselves, musta killed some other hunters, likely, and their shootin' wasn't so bad, fer Redskins. We run 'em off, finally, but they looted an' burned our outfit and killed old Charlie 'Sawlogs' Nelson, our cook. Really messed him up. Pissed off at us shootin' the hell out of 'em, I guess.

He leaned back and belched, then blew a cloud of smoke toward the ceiling. "Wasn't Blackfeet, Sioux 'er Cheyenne. Some other tribe—an' they was on the move. Lucky fer us, we never come up to 'em."

Ben motioned to the waiter for a refill and Hank waited until the man had poured their cups full.

"Anyway, she was a long trail back here without an outfit. Sleepin' on the ground under wet saddle blankets. No food but a couple deer. But here we are." He sighed, "Obliged fer the hospitality, old pard." Will echoed his thanks.

Ben relit his cigar and passed a couple more over for them.

"Well, accordin' to the Benton paper, it was likely Nez Perce. The tribe was stirred up down in Oregon by land grabbers and chased up here by the Army. They seem to have bin pretty good about not killin' civilians along the way but I s'pose, bein' as you was shootin' their buffalo, they had a mad on. Didn't help when you shot the hell out of 'em, too."

"Well, I usually make it a point to shoot back when someone's pullin' a trigger at me." Hank said sarcastically. "I notice you do the same, Ben."

"Yep. I know. Guess I just have a little sympathy for 'em, them tryin' to git their families up to Canada and be left alone, like."

He sipped his coffee and they were quiet for a spell, then Ben said, passing over the *Fort Benton Times*, "Paper says they fought a battle at the Big Hole an' killed a raft of soldiers, so now they got Gibbon, Howard and

Miles all chasin' 'em on north. Be another fight when they catch 'em, I s'pect."

He drew on his cigar and released a cloud of smoke. "So what's your plans now?"

"Right now, we got $40 between us. Not enough to do a damn thing except have a good drunk. Which I'm ready to do." Will said. "Sorry about your outfit, Ben, looks like we just ain't a good investment. We'll make it good." Hank nodded.

"How'd you boys like to take a trip down south with me? I could use some gun company an' I'll make it worth yer while. New outfits, $500 apiece and we'll call it square on the buffalo huntin' layout."

Harp came to the table and Ben introduced him.

The sheer size of the man and his wide smile made quite an impact and both men were impressed, in spite of themselves. Ben smiled.

"Harp'll be comin', too."

"What about Siccoolum? She makes a good camp tender. And a shooter, too." Hank suggested. He happened to catch the pained look that came over Ben's face at the remark and said, "What'd she do, get some sense an' head on back to her relations?"

Ben looked away. "No. She died in the spring. Consumption."

It was silent at the table. Then Hank said,

"Sorry, Ben, we hadn't heard. She was a good...a good woman. I know you were partial to her."

"Yes... I was." The words came choking out and all there knew it needed to be a closed subject. Harp was himself surprised at the emotion his boss, a hard man in many ways, displayed. *'Who was this Siccoolum?'* He and Hite had sat by quite a few campfires and talked about many things but that name had never come up.

Will asked, to change the subject. "So what's down south?"

Ben took a deep breath. "A youngster. The one the Paiutes traded to the Navajo. I want to see if we can find 'im and get him back to his people there in Harrison.

Hank looked at Will. "Navajos! That's a long way south. And ain't they still warrin' with the Army down there? Apaches, Comanches, Pimas, an' all."

"What? You boys gettin' shy, all of a sudden?" Ben said teasingly. He took a long slurp of his coffee and burned his mouth. "Damn! That's hot!"

"Should be. He just poured it." Hank grinned.

He looked at his friend and shrugged. "Why not, we don't have anythin' else goin' just now. And you wipin' the huntin' stake off, why, that alone is worth it. Right, Will?"

That worthy nodded and said,

"Well, that's settled, then. Let's drink on it."

They adjourned to the bar, Will still favoring his game leg. Harp followed them, hesitant, until Ben grabbed his arm and propelled him in, too.

Chief Joseph
courtesy of Wikipedia

CHAPTER 13.

At the ranch two days later, Harp was in the barn helping Kittledge fork hay down to the horses and asked the little man who this 'Siccoolum' was.

"Heard 'em talkin' in Benton 'bout her an' was curious." He said, leaning on his fork.

Kittledge was for once silent, his face grim as he considered his reply.

"Well, she was an Injun gal—-good looker, tall—-Gros Ventre tribe, I guess. She died of consumption this spring. It's quite a story..."

Harp was willing to listen and Kittledge, always ready to be talking, spun his yarn with only a few embellishments.

"...and Hite buried her in the Indian way, on a picane, a scaffold, up on the hill over there." He gestured to the west of them. "Shot her two horses right there below her, good ones, they was, too—-fer her to ride in the Everlastin', ye know. What Injuns call the "Shadow Land" they goes to—-kinda like our Heaven, I guess." He spit, the brown glob nearly hitting a mouse who scurried out of the way. "Good woman—-but a bloodthirsty bitch. Loved a scalp, especially offa Sioux 'er Blackfeet. Made Ben a war shirt once that was covered with them, jest covered!"

"Thought white men never took scalps?"

"Nope. Ben never did. But she took aplenty of them he shot, by God, an' not all of 'em was Injun, neither!" He spit at another, slower mouse and hit its backside, making it squeak.He chuckled, thinking,

'Scalpin' Mormons was a whole 'nother story.'

* * *

Up at the house, Ben was seated in his chair on the porch, drinking coffee that Felice had brought them. Hank, Will and Bless Ketchum were sitting taking their ease there, also. Ketchum was saying,

"...was over there yesterday and she came out with her face covered. Had a hard time talkin'. I guess he must hev hit her a lick. Big bastard! They say he's got quite a temper when he's drinkin' and he likes to gamble some, too. Lost the team you gave 'em to Bowles in a card game. S'pose Betty gave 'im Hell and he let 'er hev it."

Ben stirred and Felice came and took Daisy from him. The sleeping child was limp in her arms. He got up. "Guess I'll go over fer a visit."

The others all got up, too.

"No. You boys stay here. This is family stuff an' all I'm goin' to do is ask her if she wants to come on home." He saw the concern on Ketchum's face and said, "I'll be fine. Don't need any company."

He went down to the barn and Kittledge and Harp came down from the loft, seeing him enter.

"H'lo, boys. Thought I'd take a little ride. Monte there is gettin' fat."

Kittledge, knowing his boss by now, saw that he was upset, though he was hiding it well.

"Talked with Bless 'bout Betty, I bet. Am I right, Ben?"

"Yeah. Think I'll go over an' hev a visit with 'em. See how she's gettin' along. He told me she had her baby—a boy."

He took down Monte's bridle and stepping out the back door to the big structure, whistled and Monte came ambling over. Leading the horse in, he dropped the reins and worked a brush over its back for a little, then saddled it. Tightening the cinch, he was surprised to see Kittledge throwing leather on a little roan. "Now, Kitt, I don't need any company."

"You're gettin' it anyway." He looked at Ben defiantly. "Betty's always been...well, my favorite, ya know, Boss. An' I'm not standin' fer anyone to beat on 'er. Would have gone over earlier but the big bastard usually hez his friends around and I didn't want ole' Bless to back me. His leg an' all, ya know. 'Sides, I didn't know jest <u>what</u> to do. 'Fraid I'd end up shootin' 'im. Likely she'd just tole me to mind my own business. You bein' her paw an' all, though, that's different."

"What you wants me to do, Boss?" Harp asked.

"Just go on up to the house and take on a load of coffee, Harp. We'll be back by supper." Ben swung up and ducked his head as he exited the barn. Kittledge had to do no such thing and he followed Ben on out and into the lane.

* * *

Harp stood in the barn, undecided, when the doorway was filled with the men from the house, who busied themselves with cornering horses out in the corral, bringing them in and saddling them. Harp went over to Will.

"Thought Hite said we' was all to wait here?"

"<u>We</u> do what we want, darky. An' somethin' tells us Ben might need some help. So we're just fixin' to follow along behind, like. 'Case he gits in a jam."

"I wants to come, too, <u>whitey</u>. But none of these nags'll take my weight, I don't think."

Will looked at him. "That's likely, with the saddle horses here, but ..." He looked over at the stalls in the back of the barn. "See that big gray? Take him. His name's Atlas. He's gentle an' you kin ride him. You'll hev to ride

95

'im bareback, though. Not a saddle here that'd fit ya." He spat. Niggers was one reason the War had been fought, but in his mind, their freedom was a damn poor exchange for the deaths of so many good men.

* * *

Ben saw smoke coming from the chimney when they rode up. The hitch rail in front of the house had three horses already tied there so he got down and dropped the reins, trusting the old horse to stay. Kittledge remained on his mount and Ben saw that he'd brought his rifle along and it was out of the scabbard and across his saddle. He walked to the door and before he could open it, Blaquet pulled it to and stepped into the opening. Ben heard something going on inside but couldn't quite make it out. But he could hear Betty's voice.

"Wot yu want, eh?" His voice was slurred.

"Why, Thought I'd come visit my in-laws, Jacques. Heard Betty had a boy." Ben said easily, a smile on his face but his eyes steady and piercing.

Blaquet muttered something. "Betty, she's sick. Don't want to see anybody."

Ben stepped closer. 'She'll see her father, boy."

Blaquet blocked the door and with a quick movement, Ben brought up an arm and pushed him inside, then stepped into the room. Betty was there, and her face filled him with anger. Its right side was black and blue, with an eye nearly shut, her upper lip swollen. She stood by a crib, two babies crying in it. To the right, around a table whose top was filled with bottles, sat three young men, sullen and staring, their faces flushed with booze. Ben turned to Betty. "What happened to your face, Honey?"

Before she could answer, Blaquet stepped in front of her, a knife in his hand held low. "She don't got to talk to you! Git out!"

The other men came up from the table and one pulled a knife, also. Ben put his hands up in a placating gesture and backed slowly out the door, the others following Blaquet as they came out. Once outside, the men saw Kittledge, his rifle at the ready. Blaquet lowered his weapon as Ben said,

"Jest wanted to git you boys outside, away from Betty an' the babies, in case things got a little... risky."

Kittledge grinned.

* * *

Hank and the others thundered over the hill and across the ford up to the house, pulling up beside Ben and Kittledge's horses. Two men lay moaning in front of the house, the big one curled around his arm, which was cocked off at an angle, the other unconscious. Another was sitting by the door and the men could see, from the blood pumping over the hand that fell weakly away from his side, that he was badly hurt. As they dismounted, he fell over sideways.

From the doorway, Betty came in the act of bundling one of the babies into a blanket. She stepped over her husband, he with the hurt arm, spitting on him as she went. Kittledge followed her with his arms full of baby clothes and other items. Then Ben stepped through the entrance, another baby in his left arm, throwing coal oil into the interior and then pausing to light a match, which he flipped in. The place went up with a whoosh! The horses at the hitch rail reared back and Hank and the others were hard put to keep order. Ben saw them and said, "I'd swear I told you boys to stay home."

"Just thought you might need some company— but we see that you handled it in your usual easy manner." Will retorted. Hank went to Betty and held the baby while she clambered into the saddle of one of the horses at the rail, then she reached down and took the child from him.

Harp took the clothes from Kittledge. When he got settled in the saddle, Ben handed him the other baby.

Kitt said, "C'mon, Betty, let's head on home." The two started off. Ben watched them go,

"Since you're here, go an' let the horses in the barn out and bring 'em along. Take the bridle off those horses an' git 'em headed fer home."

"You take on all of 'em at once, Ben?" Hank asked.

"Naw, Kitt kept 'em from gangin' me and I carved on 'em one at a time. Blaquet was a pleasure. Slow and stupid. Another one skedaddled. Leave 'em lay where they are. Not worth messin' with 'em."

* * *

Down at the barn when they returned, Harp and the others were taking care of the horses. Ben had walked Betty and the babies up to the house. The men gathered around Kittledge as soon as the two left and Kitt, in his element, told them what had transpired.

"Soon as Ben got 'em out of the house, he sez to 'em, 'This is between me an' Blaquet. You others stay clear! Well, I could see they all wanted to jump him together, so I says, You men drop yer knives 'er I'll blast ye!" He chuckled at the memory.

"Well, it was lucky fer Ben I was there 'er he mighta got hisself killed, I'd say! Anyhow, they shucked their knives and Blaquet comes in swingin'. Ben jest let 'im come an' when he threw his right, Ben grabs his arm and throws 'im, follows 'im down to the ground and breaks his wing fer 'im right there! That quick! So he's out first off. Well, Blaquet's two friends don't take that too well and they both come after Ben. He lets 'em come, then grabs 'em by the head and crack! He knocks 'em together. Down they go but the one comes back up with a knife he picks up and takes a swipe at Ben, who falls back and draws his own. Say! Thet young buck got whittled on, let me tell you. While all this's goin' on, the third one runs over, gets his horse an' takes off." Kittledge laughed. "That Injun didn't want no part of ole Ben!"

* * *

The next day, Louie Gaspard and two other Metis' showed up at the ranch. Ben greeted them and they sat on the porch, a sober, grim group. Felice and Betty came out with coffee. When Louie saw her face, his own grew white.

"I point no finger, my frien'! Doin' that to his wife! He deserved wot he got! Jacques will likely nevair use that arm again. But what 'bout the other two? They were these men's sons. The one is near death."

"Then these fathers should have taught them to choose their friends better, Louie. They took up the quarrel, which was really just between me 'n Jacques. 'Course, If they want revenge fer their boys, I guess I could accommodate 'em."

He threw a cold look at them. After a moment, there was a general shaking of heads.

"Then as far as I'm concerned, the matter is settled. An' Betty an' the babies'll stay here."

The coffee was drunk in near silence and the Metis' got up to go. Louie turned at the step and raised his hand. Ben gripped it.

"Ben....I hope this don't come between us."

"Not with me, Louie, but make sure yore people know I an' mine are not to be trifled with."

"That will I!"

* * *

Betty was glad to be back home. She enlisted the help of Felice and the two each took on the baby chores,

99

leaving Kittledge and Bless to fill in where they could. Ben saw with amusement that Kittledge was eager to give Betty every consideration and wasn't surprised when she came to him and asked how she could get a divorce. She wanted no part of the man she had married. Ben scratched his head about that and finally said maybe Felice and Bless could ask old Father Dupree about it. She decided that was wise and did so. They came back with the old Father's answer, which was that Catholics were not supposed to divorce, that she was supposed to submit to being a proper wife and not anger her husband.

"The Hell with them all, then! I'm done being a Catholic!" Betty stormed.

Ben was amused. It was much the answer he expected from her. Of all the children, this girl probably had the worst temper. What did surprise him, though, was when Kittledge came and asked him diffidently if he'd mind if he and Betty 'got hitched.'

"You and Betty...!!??"

"Yessir. I know I'm too old fer her but I asked her and she said 'Yes." He shuffled his feet. " I'll treat her right, Ben. I promise you that."

"Sure...Kitt. Sure. I know you will. Well....I guess it's up to her. If she wants you, why I say, congratulations and good luck!" Thinking on it, he could remember how well the two always got along on the road trips. Maybe it would be a good match. Time would tell, he guessed. For some reason, it made him look up to the hills, where Siccoolum was.

*   *   *

There was no formal wedding but he got the two together and told them that the ranch and horses were theirs. A wedding present. Both of them looked at Ben with amazement, though on reflection both knew that

100

since Siccoolum had died, Ben wanted to be gone from the place. Betty came and hugged him.

"Where will you go, Father Ben?

"Oh...the men and I are goin' to take a trip down south. See if we can't scare up the boy that's missing from the train. Took care of the rest of 'em, but that one still bothers me. Maybe we kin find 'im. I want to at least give it a try."

Betty began to silently cry.

Ben said defensively, "Well, Seems to me, you kids is pretty well taken care of now. Katy is doin' well back East, Freddy's off with Steele, Waterwheel took off to the Crow...I'd like to see you settled, Honey, and I'll be satisfied."

Kittledge was solemn. "Ben, We'll take you up on that——I know Bless would partner up with me. We talked about it some, already."

"Then it's a done deal."

PART III

CHAPTER 14.

Ben picked out a couple young Percherons from the herd and insisted on paying Kittledge for them. The big horses were gentle like their sire and dam and Harp made friends with them easily. Finding a saddle for his huge frame was impossible though, and so Ben made up one, using Siccoolum's as a model. Covered with buffalo hide with the hair still on, it made for a comfortable ride. Ben went up to the post, bought some horses and some more pack gear, figuring a couple horses for the camp and a horse apiece for personal gear, along with three or four extras.

While there, he saw the team that Blaquet had gambled away, and bought them back, taking them to the ranch and turning them back into the pasture. He didn't want the beautiful team to be traded off to some incomers who might misuse them. Besides, they were Betty's wedding present.

While he was there, he had a talk with both traders regarding Betty, Kittledge and Bless and the ranch. His meaning was clear: leave them be, but if they should need help, he'd appreciate their aid and make it right to them down the line. Both men were agreeable. They told Ben they were planning on heading west to California soon and maybe wouldn't see him again, so goodbyes were said. Ben offered to buy the bay mare but she was part of their plans, along with the stud, for cleaning up in races out on the west coast.

* * *

Ben left old Monte in the pasture, though he nickered until they were out of sight. Brutus, seeing his friend Snake leaving, insisted on coming, too. Since the ranch had several other dogs, most sired by Brutus, Ben decided to take him along. A good guard dog wouldn't hurt on the trail. If he got foot-sore, he'd heave him up on a pack horse and let him ride.

By the time they reached Helena, the group had become an efficient team. Hank and Will took care of the horses, Ben and Harp set up the camp and did most of the cooking, Ben had decided that he wanted to find someone who was a better camp cook than they, if he could, and so at Helena, they did some looking. The quest wasn't successful there, so they went on to Dillon, where they stocked up for the long trail over the pass and down into Idaho. Still no cook.

They tackled the pass, working against the general tide of incomers, and dropped down into the Great basin, following Ben's usual routine of stopping early for the stock to rest and graze. They weren't in any real hurry, as the weather was good and there was grass along the creeks and rivers. As much as possible they wanted to keep the Mormons ignorant of their identity. Ben shaved his beard and they all kept a tight lip when they met travelers or stopped in the little villages they passed through.

They followed the Bear River a ways then detoured to the east of the Wasatchs, winding their torturous way ever south over ridges and deep cuts where no wagons could go. Several days finally found them at Pecoa, a sleepy Mormon village, where they bought supplies and then took the trail over to the Provo river. They found good grass and water, though Indian sign was plentiful. They followed the river for many miles, down to Orem and Provo finally and Utah Lake, where they intersected the main south trail that took them over the scrub cedar hills and to the Sevier River.

* * *

Harp liked traveling. Like on the boats, he was seeing some country. He liked his boss, he liked Hank and he would have liked Will, if the bastard had met him half way. As it was, the man was forever cranky, almost as if he enjoyed being hard to get along with. Harp gave up trying to be friends with him. They seemed to rub each other wrong and didn't speak to each other if they could help it. Harp knew his inexperience and watched and learned, with Ben or Hank giving an explanation for their behavior when Harp queried them.

* * *

Will was feeling the ride. It was wearing him down. His knee was giving him fits. He was in agony by the end of the day and his usual means of allying the pain through whisky, was not available to him. He'd drunk up his reserve by Provo and the whole damn Utah country was dry. No booze was sold in any of the towns or villages they came to. So, the pain made him an unpleasant companion and he knew it but couldn't help it. Mostly, he rode with the leg out of the stirrup and hanging down.

Also, he'd been trying to compose a poem about their journey but it wouldn't come. He needed alcohol to get the muse flowing. So his mind just kept coming back to the day he'd been shot, the surgeries, the constant pain. He cursed himself for getting talked into coming on such a long trip——wouldn't have, if it had been anyone but Ben who'd asked him.

So far, all he had was,

Brigham Young meets his Maker

When Brigham meets his Maker
What will the Almighty say?
Will He ask if the man
who styles himself a Christian,
never thought there'd be a
Judgment Day?

Or if the chains that bind his heart
could somehow come apart?
And then that he would see
that God's poor blameless little children
had suffered too much death and agony.

More likely, though, that He would render
Judgment loud as rolling thunder,
send his soul to Satan's Hell down under.

There, in Hades, in the fire, Lucifer
would greet him as a favored son,

Maybe the rest would come when he got some whiskey in him.

* * *

More days of incessant riding, as the general aspect of the country began changing, and the endless color and variety of the hills began assuming a dull reddish tinge and Harp and the others became aware of just how important water was. Deep seemingly inaccessible canyons showed enormous sandstone walls and they had several dry camps. Finally, the head of the Virgin River came into sight and with a sigh of relief, they made it to Parker's ranch without any trouble, as things were quiet now with the Paiutes and Poncas who had been raising hell the year before.

Riding into the place, Ben saw that the barn had been rebuilt and the outfit was looking prosperous. The tall rancher came out on the porch when they clattered in and yelled at them to go on down to the barn and his men would see to their horses.

Parker was glad to see Ben and asked about Freddy. He was elated to hear the boy had made a full recovery. If he was curious about Siccoolum, he didn't say anything, and Ben never volunteered. Over supper and coffee later on the porch, Ben told him of his intentions for the trip. Parker scratched his bristly chin. "Ya know, I do remember hearin' somethin' about a white kid 'er two being held by the Pauites."

He turned and yelled into the house, "Maria! come out here!" The matronly Mexican woman came ambling out and he gabbled at her in Spanish. She answered and he said, "Yeah, thought so. She remembers hearin' somethin', too, about a boy but she says that was months ago, mebbe he's dead by now. Hard to say. But they could have traded 'im to the Navajo, all right."

He looked at them. "Killin' off thet whole train— Hell of a thing. That's Mormons for ye. I've heard some other things over the years. Injuns aren't the only danger to beware of in this country. You'll play hell, though. Tryin' to git to the Navajos right now could git ye killed. Ye'll need to travel through Kiowa and Apache country. Both of 'em are on the war path. If'n I kin help you any, Ben, why just ask. "

"We're pretty well fixed for 'bout ever'thin' but Big Harp here, has about wore out that cockeyed saddle I made him. You wouldn't have a good man that could fix him up a better one, would you?"

"That we have, a Mex that kin make him a fine one but it'll take him a few days. That's all right. Give your horses a rest and we'll get 'em reshod fer ye. How 'bout a drink?"

* * *

They stayed at the ranch four days and in that time, Harp was presented with an excellent new saddle made to his and his horses' larger requirements, while the horses all sported new shoes and their ribs had filled out some on the grazing along the river. Parker was a good host and his Mexican women good cooks, though the food was strange and had a heat to it from the peppers they used. Will thought it likely had something to do with keeping the food from spoiling. Their stomachs would get used to it, Parker asserted, and they might even come to prefer it. "I do, I know. I miss the Mex food when I go back east. Nothin' has any taste to it."

He wouldn't take any money for the saddle, the shoeing and the hospitality.

"Naw. Go find thet pore kid and bring 'im back to his family, Ben. Likely though, he'll be a little Redskin by now, if he ain't dead. Injuns all treat kids pretty well, if they don't knock 'em in the head right away, an' pretty soon, they're part of the tribe."

He came off the porch and held out his hand.

"Stop back and we'll hev another visit. Don't see enough people way out here."

"That we will, God willin'." Ben shook hands and they rode on out to the south.

* * *

Ben had never been farther than Parker's and had taken time to query him about the country to the south. The rancher himself had scant information to give him, so he enlisted the help of some of his older Mexican riders who had been that way. The result was a crude map that, because of the water holes, led off to the south east to where they would finally intersect the Colorado River.

108

The trail for now led through a deep long gorge cut by the Virgin River, a deep winding one that made them all uneasy. It held many spots for ambush and Ben, cautious as ever, scouted each one or relied on Hank or Will to do it. They would leave Paiute country when they got through the gorge, but then they were in an area frequented by the Kiowa or Comanche, tribes that had never been friendly to the white man.

* * *

Coming out of Utah, Will was about to go stark, raving mad from the pain and lack of alcohol. When they reached Parker's, though, that changed. Parker was no Mormon and he liked his whiskey, or if not available, tequila. That drink was new to Will but he took to it like a duck to water. Out of the saddle, with the pain relieved, and some days to drink and his leg to recuperate, he experienced a mood change that puzzled Harp. Instead of calling him 'Darky' or 'Nigger' he actually used his given name and initiated a conversation about the new saddle. Man! What a change! Harp was not one to pack a grudge and met him half-way.

Both Ben and Hank knew Will's problem and made sure that the pack horses carried plenty of tequila. In addition, Ben had talked Parker out of some laudanum, just in case. Both men knew just how their friend was hurting and though their sympathy didn't show, they still felt it. Harp figured it out finally, also.

Canyon de Chelly - Courtesy of Wikipedia

CHAPTER 15.

In New York, Katy was deeply immersed in her studies, just getting to the point to where she felt adequate in the classes. Her floor work in the hospital was no problem, and neither were the labs. She wasn't squeamish, having helped around the ranch, doctoring horses, helping during lambings, calvings and foalings. The sight of blood, even if it were human, didn't make her feel faint or throw up, as it did some of the students. The two doctors had both voiced their approval, saying she had a knack, to her delight.

Her major problem now was that one of the several male students had fallen for her and she didn't like him. She was flattered, at first, by his attentiveness, but it soon grew wearisome. He was just too pushy, too aggressive, too sure of himself. Finally, it had come to a head, when he'd gotten drunk and forced himself into her little apartment.

The splintering of the door jamb as he heaved on it, refusing to accept her demand to be left alone, was followed by a shot and a howl. She had grabbed the little pistol Ben had given her and cocking it, waited until she had a clear shot, then triggered a round that took him high in the leg, dropping him in the doorway, where he lay bleeding until the policeman on his beat, hearing the gunfire, came on the run and carted him away. Katy herself would have left him to bleed. She had little sympathy for the man and went down the next day and signed a complaint against him. Breaking and entering and attempted assault earned him jail time and dismissal from the school, with everyone saying 'good riddance.' He was a spoiled rich man's son who had not been liked.

The fact of Katy capably wielding a pistol, though, had a dampening effect on any prospective suitors, which Katy didn't mind at all. She was busy.

* * *

Back home, Betty was her amiable self again, with Kittledge an attentive husband and a familiar companion. The house rang with their laughter. She loved her two babies, and thought she might be pregnant again, to Kittledge's joy. He was hoping for a little girl.

The Metis' left them alone and he and Bless had put up their hay with the help of a couple men who had stopped on their way home, looking for work after going broke in the mines. They were good help and when the crop was up, had accompanied Bless to Fort Benton for supplies and to sell a couple teams. The two hands were paid off and caught a steamer downriver.

The big horses were at a premium and he'd returned with money and an abundance of groceries for the winter. Steele and Freddy had come through several times and each time, had news for them of Waterwheel, who had taken to the Crow way of life and had already been on a war party against the Sioux. He was now a warrior, having proved himself by stealing some horses and killing a Sioux brave. He sent his greetings to them, as did Takes His Enemy's Gun.

* * *

Harp was a good listener and what he heard around the campfires as these men talked was interesting. Ben was an uneducated man but full of common sense and

112

intelligence, experienced in the ways of men and what they would do, even Indians. When he talked, it was worth listening to. Hank had been a farmer all his life, except for the war, but those five years had hardened him and given him a perspective that made him resigned to the fact that no one got out of life alive. Through it all, though, he'd kept his sense of humor. His stories were more often funny than not. His friendship with Will and Ben seemed about all he really took serious.

Will was an educated man who likely would have been a lawyer, a professor, maybe, if the war hadn't changed him so and made him a restless vagabond who wouldn't——or couldn't, settle down and live a normal life, with a wife and family. Harp enjoyed it when Will spoke, as he thought deeper, and saw maybe farther into things than the other two, though he was not the talker that Hank was. And he used big words sometime that Harp didn't know but liked to hear, rolling them around in his mind the next day, as he did the ideas that the campfire jawing brought forth. It made the day pass more swiftly, and so the time went, as the miles passed.

Harp didn't know why *he* was there. River man Harp! Riding a horse as big as he was! Big Harp, boss of any boat crew he was in. He guessed they were about as far from the Missouri or the Mississippi as they could get, right now, and still going down deeper into this land of heat and rock. The heat seemed to lean into you. 'Must be what Hell felt like.' he thought.

What *had* happened, he knew, was seeing Hite face up to that crowd of French trappers at Fort Union, then take on the leader and carve his initial in the man's forehead. Harp had watched it but he had trouble taking it in. The man surely had a big set of balls on him. Then, later, Hite had asked Harp if he wanted to work for him. Not in any biggity way—-just up and asked Harp man-to-man, giving him some respect. What else could he say, but **'yes**?'

So here he was. But, he was getting paid good money and the job damn sure hadn't been boring, so far. And he'd learned to shoot his new rifle and pistol, given him by this man, his boss. He smiled, thinking of what Coley and Rupe and the others would say could they see him. Laugh! God, they would laugh.

* * *

One thing Ben liked about the trip from the start was the singing at the evening campfire. Harp: the man had such a voice on him that the trees shook their leaves and the ground seemed to vibrate. And he could remember songs, knew all the river ones and lots of southern ones, though he was a little light on the northern ballads. Ben's voice was mediocre, Hank's not much better, but Will had a strong tenor and together, he and Harp sure made some music worth listening to.

But through most of Utah, out of booze, Will was hurting from his knee and just too grouchy to sing much. Now, though, with whiskey and tequila along, a few drinks after supper and Will and Harp would sometimes get going and then the evenings were something to look forward to. And it was good for Will. Their poet had a dead sweetheart buried in his heart. Ben remembered the details from the war days. She'd died of Cholera back home while they were fighting at Fredricksburg. That had burned much of the fun out of the man. That and the damn war.

Hell, it was good for *him*, with Siccoolum still walking her black horse alongside his shadow. Shadows that seemed deeper and blacker down here in the desert sun. His dreams, too, were unpleasant ones. The proximity of that picane so close to the ranch had combined with Moira's house and those memories to weigh on him heavily. He'd <u>had</u> to get away from the ranch and chasing after the lost boy was a good excuse. Plus, it was something he likely couldn't do alone, so it made sense to bring the others along. Hank and Will were lost souls, anyway. Harp, he wasn't sure about. The black man just had a presence that Ben liked. He was solid, just inexperienced. Always smiling, always cheerful, and this was what the group badly needed.

* * *

And now, they were in country strange to them all. High mesas with pines and scrub cedar alternated with sagebrush and greasewood flats, cut by washes with cactus of different types, even some as tall as trees. Water was a major problem and they were relieved when they came to a little river, dry in places, in others just tiny mossy ponds.

They filled their water bags by digging a hole some ten feet from a slimy pond and bailing it until it was clear, then consulted the map. Sixty miles southeast was the Colorado River. There were seeps and other little watering places across there, but they might be hard to find and not always reliable. A big old mesa, though, almost due east, was a landmark about half way there. At its base, there was supposed to be a spring with good water. Parker's old Mex had recommended they travel that stretch at night, to save the horses and hopefully avoid hostiles, to steer by the stars and the lay of the land. They did so.

They approached the mesa cautiously. Any water hole out here meant other travelers could be there or watching it. Some little animals that looked like pigs and ran in packs took off at their approach. Ben had cautioned no shooting, but they were tempting, since the jerky was gone. The last of the water had been split between the horses. The men rode with mouths that were parched, their lips cracked and bleeding. But the spring was there, with water so cold it made their teeth hurt and they made camp and after some scouting, built a small fire and fried up some bread and beans with the last of the bacon grease,

115

washed down with black coffee. Far off, almost at the horizon, Ben, with his glasses, could see a line of green—likely the river. The next night, they went on.

The Colorado River was low and after following it downstream a mile or more, they found a crossing that had been used fairly recently. It looked deep and the water roiled slowly along, sullen, menacing. A dangerous river. Ben didn't admit it, but it scared him, made him shiver as he looked at it.

"Snake's a good water horse. I'll try it first. The big buckskin is another pretty good horse in water, so put him in if I get across okay and chouse the rest of the pack horses in to follow him. Then you boys come. Harp, you do like we said. Slip on off your horse and catch his tail. Watch his feet and he'll take you on across."

Ben took off his boots and tied them to the saddle, then loosened his cinch so the horse could breathe as he swam. The others did the same and they also loosened the pack saddles a trifle. If a horse couldn't breathe, he couldn't swim.

Snake took to the water, Brutus right behind him, and Ben let the horse have his head. The water deepened and soon they were swimming, the current stronger than Ben liked, with some undercurrents he could feel. With that, his angle changed and they came out farther downstream than he wanted, where the bank was steeper. Still, Snake heaved up it, Ben followed, Brutus came out just below them and they walked dripping back to the spot directly across from the others. He motioned them up stream and they took his meaning and so hit the water at a better angle, which put them out almost where he was waiting. Ben was glad that they had hit it when it was low.

The river would be impassable when it was high and roiling.

CHAPTER 16.

On the other side, the trail led up out of the canyon and onto a wide plateau where they could see for miles. Ben and the others wondered just where all the Indians had gone off to. They'd seen signs and glimpsed some horses but Ben thought that they were wild, though it was hard to believe any could survive in the harsh land.

The old Mex back at Parker's, Juan Morales, had told them that there was a big canyon far to the east of the river that was the heart of the Navajo country. Cajon de Chelly, he'd called it. There, they had water to irrigate their corn and gardens, as the tribe was not really by nature, nomadic. They had summer range and winter range for their flocks of sheep and goats and horses and went back and forth between them.

The summer range was on the flat desert plateaus by the canyons and their gardens and orchards stretched along the waterways there. When hot weather and fall came and the grass began to give out, they started migrating to their winter range in the higher pine forested mesas where they had built stout earthen homes they called hogans. With wood and water available, along with feed for their stock, and game, they subsisted well, most years.

* * *

The Civil War had seen the withdrawal of troops from the frontier. Their departure had left the way open to the devastation of the country, as the southern tribes saw an opportunity to push the newer white invaders out. Most of the raids against the white settlers were done by the roaming Apache or Comanche bands, but the Navajo were also involved. Many white invaders during the Gold Rush in California had pushed through their country, shooting their game, stealing from their flocks and gardens. Retaliation had been only natural and it had escalated from there. Then, the Civil War had come and they had gone on the warpath with the other tribes.

It was the young men, who got restless and sometimes went on the war trail, raiding the Mexican country to the south and bringing back captives, and usually more horses, that caused the trouble. There was perpetually a state of war that existed between the Mexicans and the Indian tribes of the region for several hundred years and Juan's and the other Mexican's description of the Navajo tribe was laced with hatred of the red man. The Civil War gave these young warriors an opportunity to strike the vulnerable white men, also.

Several punitive expeditions had subsequently been sent against all the tribes, with General Carleton, a notable strategist, being tasked with the subjugation of the red man in the south. He was successful but it was to take years past the close of the Civil War to finally achieve victory over the Apaches as they were so mobile and their livelihood depended entirely on looting and pillaging. They ranged from deep in Mexico to the Colorado River and beyond in their forays. The Comanche and Kiowa were much the same as the free ranging Apaches.

The Navajo were different, as the bulk of the tribe largely depended on their flocks and their gardens in the canyons. They were fighters, though, and a series of battles were indecisive until Kit Carson and his intrepid

1st Cavalry New Mexican volunteers came on the scene. He instituted a scorched earth policy against the tribe, burning the forage, killing the flocks of sheep, even the horse herds, destroying the gardens and of course, killing Indians as his scouts found them.

Finally, Carson and his troops overran the main Navajo stronghold in Canyon de Chelly. There, they captured many women and children, a majority of the tribe's last horse herd, and after a pitched battle, broke the tribe's resistance and they surrendered.

The Navajo were banished from their land to a temporary imprisonment in a concentration camp setting at Fort Defiance in Arizona. Mistreatment was the rule there and their desperate plight continued: they were ordered on an exodus across mountains and deserts, a 180 mile trek which came to be known as the 'Long Walk' to Fort Sumner in New Mexico.

It was March and the weather was cold and many of the poorly clad and fed exiles died along the way.

At Fort Sumner, firewood was scarce, the alkaline water of the Pecos River made them sick and they had to share the forty square mile reservation with the Apache. With no materials to build shelters, they were forced to dig into the ground and live like gophers. They were supposed to become farmers but in the sterile ground, no corn would grow. They existed there for three years, then General Sherman came on a fact finding mission and reported the plight of the Navajo to Congress, who relented and, in 1868, signed a treaty with the Navajo that gave them the largest Indian reservation in America, the 3.5 million acre 'Big Rez', *Dinetah*, their homeland, a desert land that the whites considered worthless.

* * *

When the tribe returned to their homeland, they found everything destroyed. For years, then, the *Dineh* had

119

to exist as best they could as the government, recuperating from the War, gave them little, slowly rebuilding their flocks and gardens and regaining some prosperity (some of it coming from the Mexicans in raids south). During this whole time, many of the Comanche, Apache and Kiowa were still out, still hostile and often preying now upon the Navajo themselves for subsistence.

With the Navajo's original numbers, had they a strong war leader to unite them, they could have caused the army a great deal more trouble. Now, when Ben and his party came on the scene, the tribe's status was 'defeated but not tame'. But where were they? The country seemed empty.

CHAPTER 17.

Will saw them first. He was scouting forward on a ridge and with Ben's other glasses, glimpsed a little flock of sheep over on a wooded side hill tended by a couple young kids who were likely Navajo, as the other tribes, from what they knew, didn't mess with livestock, other than to eat them when they were raiding. He watched awhile, and presently a man rode up to them out of a coulee on their far right. He was armed with a bow and arrows. He had brought them something to eat and they sat and talked while they ate.

Behind Will, the rest of the men caught up to him and waited below until he came down to them and told them what he'd been looking at.

Now they had to make contact with them. Not for the first time, Ben wished that Siccoolum was there. He only knew a little sign. The others had none. At Ben's direction, they waited while he showed himself, walking his horse slowly forward, with a tree branch in his hand. Brutus was on a rope held by Harp, as the dog, evidently considering it his duty, had taken on and whipped about every dog in every village they'd gone through and Ben had no intention of letting him come along and make a great impression by maiming or killing the sheep dogs guarding their flock.

121

He went forward, waving the branch above his head and the horseman watched him come, then mounted and came to meet him.

Ben saw he was a well set up man of strong features and graying hair, shoulder length but not braided, tied with a red and blue band. He wore a breechclout, leggins and moccasins and rode the pinto horse with only a blanket for a saddle and a small braided rope that was looped around the horse's lower jaw. Except for the bow, he was unarmed. He stopped and raised his hand and Ben did likewise, then spoke the only Navajo he'd gleaned from Morales: *"Yaa' eh tieh"* (hello)

The Indian sat his horse and looked at Ben, then at his back-trail, muttered a guttural equivalent to what Ben had just said, and lifted his eyebrows and rubbed his hand in a circular scrubbing motion, palm forward, in a questioning way. Ben correctly guessed he was asking if there were any others and held up three fingers, then tucking the branch under his arm, clasped his hands in the universal signal for friendship. He then kneed Snake forward and held out his hand, nodding his head. Hesitating again, the Indian finally took his hand and they shook.

Meanwhile, the boys, seeing him come, had gathered their flock and with the dogs helping, had hurried them back over the hill. Ben, not knowing what else to do, made the sign he remembered for eating, merely a passing of the hand repeatedly toward his mouth, then the question sign: palm forward and in a circle. The Indian was clearly reluctant, but finally motioned to him to come, to follow him, and Ben waved at the others to follow them.

CHAPTER 18.

Hosteen Yaazi, for Ben later found that was the man's name, led them a mile back through the pines into a small ringed group of seven or so small brush shelters, smoke curling up from several of them, with children running out to see the procession as it came in to the irregular circle. Against a low sandstone wall, a small spring was surrounded by a splash of green, its water coming up to the surface and going back down after a short run, into the sandy ground.

It was primitive. Women peeped out from under open brush arbors beside the shelters, drawn away from their work where they were spinning yarn or tending looms where blankets or clothes were being woven, their bright colors showing in the dim light under the shaded structures. Dogs were underfoot and came out to bark. Horses stood by the entrances of several of the homes, tied or hobbled. Colts were here and there, dragging halter ropes. Some others, young yearlings or two year olds, were being ridden by children, who seemed to be the ones breaking them to ride and be handled.

Ben, seeing that, thought it a good process, but wondered about them getting hurt. All heads turned to watch the *Bilaganna*, the hated white man, riding in, invading the sanctity of their village.

They came to a stop by a shelter not different or any bigger than any of the others. Beside it, under an arbor, was a woman who came forth and without speaking, gazed on the sight of four white men, led in by her husband.

The Navajo flew between them for a bit, the woman clearly upset, the only word that Ben caught of the exchange being *"yiya"* which, he thought maybe meant 'eat' or 'food.' He got down and going to the buckskin's packs, he rummaged and brought forth one of his trade goods, a small silver bell. He carried it over and presented it to her, ringing it as he went. Her hands came up to cup it and her eyes widened.

Clearly, it was something new that intrigued her. From all sides, children came, shyly sidling up, to see what it was that was making the musical sound. Delighted, she rang it for them and nodding at Ben, she disappeared into the shelter. Ben gestured to the others, and they brought forth little gifts, too, for Hosteen Yaazi. Hank gifted him a folding barlow knife, Will, a bright silk scarf, Harp, a brass belt buckle. Ben had bought trade goods as he thought of them, trying to keep them small but useful or intriguing, portable. He had found the bells in Helena and bought a dozen of them, as he had the scarves and buckles of various types.

Along with such things, he had loaded up on coffee, flour and sugar, always good trade items. The best of them, he would save for the possible trade for the boy.

Now, their host had seated them on beautiful rug blankets under the arbor and his wife had brought them cold water from the spring in a heavy olla, pouring for them into smaller pottery mugs that she handed around. The water was cold and tasted slightly of iron. The men nodded, smacked their lips and said, "Good, good."

About then, Brutus had had enough of the smelling about him and took after some of the curious dogs, making a row. Hosteen Yaazi smiled and said, *"Leeechaa, Leechaa"* and growled, the sound a perfect imitation of

Brutus's deep growl. The men laughed, but Harp, tasked with making sure Brutus stayed on his best behavior, got up and tied him closer in to them where they could watch to see he didn't abuse the fragile hospitality.

As the woman brought out food and served them, Ben saw her eyes widen as she took in Hank's freckled face. There was fear there. Did she think he was disease ridden? She nor any of the Navajo had likely never seen a freckled white man, let alone a black man like Harp.

"They think you might be sick, Hank, with all those freckles on you. Laugh a little and try to scrub 'em off fer 'em. Maybe they kin see they're in the skin and don't come off."

He did and the tension lessened a little, though Ben, trying to see them all as they must look to a man who hadn't any much to do with white men, could see that all the strangeness wasn't on the side of the Navajo. There were two very unfamiliar races meeting here, three if one included Harp.

For their part, the Navajo food was strange. Flat coarse corn flour cakes with beans and some other stuff—- shredded boiled meat—-mutton, Ben thought, with some of the peppers sliced up like the Mexicans used in their cooking. Hosteen Yaazi took his, rolled it and dipped it in a bowl full of red sauce and brought it to his mouth, gesturing to them to partake. They did, and it was good, though very hot to the taste of Northerners who were used to blander fixings.

* * *

They sat amiably, the food and the heat making them drowsy and the lack of a common language making communication tough. Presently, Ben brought forth a cigar and lighting it from the fire, he drew a few puffs, then handed it around. Yaazi watched the men as they drew smoke in and blew it out, then, when his turn came,

125

did the same. He coughed and his eyes watered. None of the others paid any attention. The cigar was smoked to its tiny end.

Finally, Ben made a repeated gesture of sleeping——closing his eyes and laying his head down on his hands and then sweeping an arm about. Yaazi interpreted it correctly: a place to camp. He got up and led them out of the village and back from where they had come to a flat, grassy spot. He indicated that they should set up there and so they threw down the packs, off-saddle and hobbled the horses and turned them out to graze. Then, the men turned to and built their own brush arbor, using cedar trees for posts and cross pieces and pine boughs criss-crossed and tied in place for the roof.

The only thing they were lacking was water, and their water bags would have to do for now. The horses would graze and be watered that night, then go on a stay-line between two trees. Ben thought they should still stand guard over the camp and so they kept on their regular routine, splitting the duty as always.

* * *

They stayed in camp there two days, being visited at times by Yaazi, usually in the company of another brave or two, never more. The women and children stayed away. Each time, they offered them coffee heavily laced with sugar. Then they would smoke a cigar. This was a hit with the men and they expressed their pleasure by bringing them meat and other food, usually the flat tortillas or sauces. Ben responded by bringing in a deer he'd shot and that was well received. Otherwise, the men rested in camp and discussed their options.

* * *

The third evening, Harp and Will were singing when Yaazi showed up. He sat and Ben poured him coffee and offered the sugar bowl. Yaazi nodded and Ben took a spoon and stirred in a helping. Yaazi never took his eyes from the men, particularly Harp, who was hitting some low notes in *'Sweet Chariot'*. He sat there until they stopped and then waved his hand, asking for more. They gave him a rousing rendition of *"Wait for the Wagon"* complete with Hank and Will doing a two-step sort of marching dance that made him laugh with delight. It was late when they stopped and indicated they were going to turn in. Ben noticed that Yaazi saw Will take his rifle and post himself as guard by the horses before the man left for the village.

* * *

It was the middle of the next day and Ben was trying to decide just what they should do when Yaazi came walking into camp with a young woman. They greeted each other in the way that had become habit—-handshake and smiles all around. Ben offered them coffee and of course, it was accepted. Then they sat and the day became brighter when the young woman said in English,

"I am Notsa Begay. Hosteen Yaazi sent for me after you came. He asks me to interpret for you. If you wish it, I will tell him you agree." Her voice was pitched low and it had a somewhat guttural quality to it that made it a little hard to understand but Ben was relieved just the same. Now, they were getting somewhere!

He nodded and smiled. "We would surely like that, Miss Begay. It's been hard, trying to get across to Yaazi what we came all this way for. My name is Ben Hite. These others here..." He introduced the men and they greeted her enthusiastically, as happy as Ben was to hear English coming from a Navajo.

"Is Yaazi the chief hereabouts?" Ben asked, while Harp was pouring coffee and getting the sugar cup going around.

"Hosteen Yaazi is...well, the head man, I guess you could say, of the Bitter Water clan. We Dinee' as we call our tribe, don't really have one main chief. We are made up of clans: the Bitter Water clan, the Mud clan, the Turning Mountain clan, Slow talking clan, the Yucca Fruit clan and some others. Usually, a man is the head of the clan——but not always, sometimes it's a woman. Sometimes, it's a couple elders, men or women. It depends. Here, though, it is Hosteen Yaazi."

She sipped her coffee and looked at Ben through dark eyes that reminded him forcibly of another woman's. Her oval face was handsome, even pretty, with dusky fine skin and straight brows, a full mouth and brilliant white teeth that flashed as she spoke. She was, Ben thought, in her middle twenties, a tall, slender woman, poised and confident. And intelligent, from her shrewd look about her as she had come into camp. That one look had taken in and digested everything, he felt. He wondered how to go about this, now that she was there.

"First, I would like you to tell Yaazi that we have come in peace and wish only to ask him if he knows the answer to a question. If he can help us, we offer gifts."

She looked at him. "A question about gold, I suppose. That seems to be the usual reason for you white men to venture so far into our land."

He shook his head. "No, this is not about gold. But to get you to understand, I need to tell you and him a story."

That got her attention and he commenced to relate the story of the Perkins train and how he came to know about it. The telling took time and more coffee, and he talked slow, so that she could keep up with the telling to Yaazi, who listened attentively.

* * *

128

....so, we came hopin' that we could find and bring the boy back to his people up north. And we're askin' Yaazi...and you, fer help." He finished up.

Talking so much had made his throat dry and he got up and took a big drink from a water bag hanging from one of the nearby trees. Sitting back down, he said, "So what does he think? Does he know of the boy and will he tell us, or did we come all this way for nothin'?"

She finished translating and sat sipping her cold coffee, looking at him. Ben sat back, wondering about her. 'Her English was good. Where had she learned it?' Hard on that, came the thought: wonder if she's married.' Now, where had <u>that</u> come from, he wondered?

'A white man that don't care about the yellow metal,' she thought. How different he is. <u>If</u> he tells the truth.' She knew, her tribe all knew, that white men were notorious liars. Not for nothing were they likened to the snake's slithery movement or Coyote's evil doings. They said one thing and did or meant another. "Watch their mouths," High Walker Nez had told her. "Whatever comes out of it is surely a lie."

"Yaazi says that he doesn't know of any boy such as you talk of, but if you would stay here awhile, he would get word out to a crystal gazer he knows, who maybe can find him for you."

"A crystal gazer?"

"A person, a shaman, who can see into his crystal and find things for people. This man would need to be paid for this."

"I could do that. Ask him to...what? Ask this crystal gazer to come and to find the boy."

Navajo talk: the sound of the language, with its unknown meanings and nuances jarred on Ben. He forced himself to take an easy strain, just sit back and let her do her work. He thought she would need some payment too, for the interpreting. What would she like, he wondered?

Yaazi got up and with a wave, headed back to his village. She got up to follow.

"Yaazi is going to send for him. I told him that you would pay the man when he came. Maybe tomorrow." She walked away. Ben and the other men watched her go.

"Quite a woman," Hank remarked, idly, but with a look at Ben.

"Yeah. Wonder where she learned English."

"Damn good for us, I'm thinkin'."

CHAPTER 19.

A day passed with no visitors. Ben took his ease as did the other men. It had been a long journey and the days were hot and conducive to lazying about.

The next day, early, Yaazi and Notsa came to the camp with an old man. She introduced him. "This is Kinlichee Nakai. He is a *Hataalii*. I guess that translates to a medicine man, in English. He is a crystal gazer and says he will find the boy for you, if he is alive yet and on the land of our fathers. He asks for a silver bell like the one you gave to Tsosie and a cup of the sweet stuff—sugar."

"Yes, we can do that." Ben said.

He went and got a bell and made up a pouch of the sugar for the old man, putting both by him on the ground where he was seated, drinking his coffee. The old shaman grunted, looking Ben in the eyes intently.

Presently, he took his crystal, a large flake of translucent mica, from the little sack he carried. Laying it on a small badger hide, he brought forth another little pouch and took some powder from it. This he sprinkled on the flake, chanting as he did, then he picked the crystal up and looked into it, holding it nearly into the sun first, then turning it in a circle to all the directions.

He put the flake back down on the hide, folded it over and tucked it back into his bag, then gestured for more coffee. Ben poured for him and offered the cup of sugar. The old man put two heaping spoons in and slurped, then spoke in Navajo. Notsa listened, then reported,

"He says the boy is presently with the Yucca Fruit clan over in Chinle Canyon. He is the property of Pinto Keeyani. At the changing of the moon, they will be holding a *Hozhoji Hatal,* a Blessing Way chant for his son at the foot of the Black Mesa. At Wolf Spring."

"So he's alive and with this clan?" 'Had the old shaman known where the boy was or had the crystal really told him? It was a question Ben would have given money to have answered.'

"Yes."

"How far is this Chinle Canyon? Could we go to it without starting a war or something?"

"East about three days ride. Yes, you could go if you had a guide——I could go with you but I would have to get some one of the tribe to go along. It wouldn't be... acceptable if I went alone with you. You will need an interpreter, anyway, and I...have nothing to hold me." Ben wondered about that but let it go.

"You'd do this? Trust us?"

"Nakai says you are a good man. Yaazi says the same. Yes, I will trust you. I want to go there, anyway."

"When do you want to leave?"

"Tomorrow we could go. I will need to pay Hosteen Yaazi for a horse and what I need. Another bell, a buckle and some sugar and coffee would do it."

"Is that enough for a Navajo horse?"

"It doesn't have to be one of his best."

"Yes, it does. We want our interpreter to be well mounted. You'll need two. One to pack your things. I have something that he will like. We'll go pick out your horses and do some tradin'."

He went to the packs and pulled some things from one and put them in a sack.

They walked into the Navajo circle and to Yaazi's, where he was sitting in the shade. At his invitation, they sat and Ben lit a cigar with a match he struck with his thumbnail, making them blink. Matches were another unknown. Fire from a little stick! He offered it to Yaazi and to Notsa. Each puffed until the cigar was consumed.

"Tell him we'd like to trade for a couple of his best horses." Ben directed her. She did so.

"He likes his horses, he says they are his friends. They wouldn't like to leave him, he says. He asks, though, what do you have to trade?"

For answer, Ben reached in a sack and pulling out a fine pair of scissors, took a piece of hide and made a straight cut. Yaazi's eyes narrowed. He called out and Tsosie came to watch as Ben made another cut. Both women covered their mouths in awe and Ben handed them to her, showing her how to hold them. Then he reached in his bag again and pulled out a small telescope. He extended it and, holding it to his eye, turned the ocular a little, sharpening the focus, then handed it to Yaazi. "Tell him to point it at the far mountain, never at the sun. The sun would hurt his eye, blind him."

She did so, and he gingerly held the scope to his eye and awkwardly pointed it toward a far mountain. Then he nearly dropped it as his eye evidenced the magnification and the mountain came near. His eyes got large. Ben smiled.

CHAPTER 20.

Notsa came the next day riding a good looking grulla and leading a lightly packed pinto, the one that Yaazi had been riding the day that Ben first saw him. With her were two older Navajo Ben had never seen before, the bigger one with a scar on his face was Nakleetsa Jesho, the other, younger man was Nascha Bisti. Both carried bows and quivers of arrows. They rode horses a cut below either one of Notsa's and seemed a little ashamed of the fact. They led another old mare with a young colt alongside. She carried their bedrolls. They were ready and the day's ride to the east began.

Jesho led the way, with Nascha Bisti following him, then Notsa. After her, Ben rode Snake, with the others strung out behind. The day was hot and the sky clear, except for some circling buzzards or eagles far out ahead of them.

Hours into the day, they held up at a small seep Jesho led them to and let the horses drink after they had filled their water bags and ollas the Navajos had strapped on their horses. They rested there through the heat of the day and Ben made a small fire of dead twigs and brewed a pot of coffee. All partook and after Ben passed out some jerky, the men settled back to nap. Ben stayed awake and alert, his rifle in his lap. Presently, Notsa came and sat by him. Curious, he asked her where she had learned her English.

"My mother and I were part of the Bitter Water clan who were captured by the Texas Militia when we went to visit relatives down by the Zuni Mountains. They took us back to Austin and my mother was sold to John Holden, a rancher.

We lived in his hacienda. My mother was a slave there. She worked in the kitchen and had to visit his bed when he wanted her. I was sent to help the Catholic priest, Father O'Hearn. He was a good man. He kept school for the rancher's children and I attended at his insistence. I ran away to the church after my mother killed herself. I was twelve and Holden was going to take me into his bed that night. He and my mother argued and she took up a gun, shot him, then herself. Father O'Hearn had me taken back to my people when they were at Bosque Redondo."

She looked at Ben and then away out to where the eagles and buzzards were circling, some miles away yet. "Something is dead out there."

That evening, the heat dissipated somewhat, the party found out what it was. Lying in a small wash, were five dead and scalped Navajos, their bodies showing the effects of the scavengers hunger.

"Looks like a family: man, woman, an older boy and two kids, boy and a girl," Hank said.

The Navajos wouldn't go near the bodies. "Chindis!" they repeated over and over.

Notsa explained, "Chindi means spirit, evil spirit. Ghosts walking. Especially when the bodies are not properly buried."

"Want us to bury them?" Ben asked.

"No! Come away! You can do nothing now."

* * *

Later, at the camp that night, after a frugal supper of tortillas, beans and the last of a ripe haunch of venison, Ben asked, "So who do you think might have done it?"

136

The answer surprised him. Notsa hesitated, then said, "White or Mexican scalpers. The Mexican government still pays a hundred dollars a scalp for Indian scalps." She shivered. "They are well armed and come from either Mexico or Texas or both to do their killing. Many Navajo, Hopi, Apache, Pima and Zuni have been killed by these bands of scalpers."

"How many of them were there?"

"Nakleetsa thinks a dozen. He thinks we should go back. They may be ahead of us."

Ben walked over to the others and appraised them of the situation as she had told him.

"I'd like to keep going. Maybe we can put these bastards under. If we do, I'd say the Navajo might have reason to think more kindly of us. But Jesho wants to turn back. Can't blame him, I guess. All they got are bows and these scalpers have guns."

"You got a plan?" Hank asked.

"Well, sort of...." He explained to them what he wanted to do and they agreed.

Will said, "Might work, but I doubt that Jesho wants to risk their scalps——especially when he's never seen us shoot."

"We'll see. They must hate these bastards."

Walking back to the Navajos, he said, "You hate these men and what they've been doing here in your country?" They agreed vehemently that the scalpers were 'monsters' walking the *Dinetah*."

"Then you kin help us git rid of them."

"What can we do? There are twelve of them and just four of you with guns. We have only our bows and our arrows." Jesho said through Notsa, looking at the ground.

"Still, that is good and will help us. Here is what we will do...."

* * *

137

Amos Fleck opened his eyes on what was to be his last day on earth thinking that they just needed two more scalps to make it a round two dozen and that meant $2400.00, payable in Mex gold, which added to the eight hundred they had already, meant each man's share of the money was better than two hundred and sixty dollars. Damn good wages when a man only made a dollar a day punching cows or maybe two bucks shoveling ore. He liked buffalo hunting but Injuns were a lot easier to skin and you needed a lot less gear to haul around.

'Damn, it was good that the Army had taken all the guns the Navajo had. It made it a lot safer hunting when they just had arrows to throw at you. Like that poor damn brave who'd shot all his at them after Bone had killed his two kids.'

He rolled out of his blanket and nudged Kiley, the one eyed redhead sleeping next to him. He came up with a grunt and together, the two stood a little ways out from the other sleepers and watered the ground. Then Fleck turned and hollered, "C'mon, boys! Git yer asses off the ground! Sun's up!"

The sleeping figures began moving, and soon a fire was going and rancid bacon was sizzling in the pan. They'd been out for three weeks now, and this was the last of the fourth slab. Soon they'd be eating their boot straps unless they could get a deer or a javelina or two.

Bone had wanted to cut some hams off the last Indians but Fleck had said that maybe that could wait until they got a little hungrier. Truth was, he'd eaten redskin meat before, and he thought it had made him sick. No, he'd wait awhile. But if nothing else showed up, why then, maybe the old gut would be ready for it.

Horses showed the effects, too, of constant riding and the heat. They needed some days of good grazing but this ground, nearly desert, was sparse, and the Navajo flocks had left little grass. They'd keep on heading east, toward what Handley said was the center of the Navajo

138

country. Not too close. A few more scalps, then back south, and payday.

That brought on thoughts of Carmelita, the cute little Mex whore. She was a money hungry little bitch and she'd squeal when she saw his fists full of it. What a time they'd had when he'd won that money in the big poker game! Those miners had for sure thought he never had the straight flush. He swung into the saddle and the other men, a hard-bitten crew of cutthroats and outlaws, mounted also and followed their leader east.

* * *

An hour from their morning camp, Fleck cut a fresh trail—three or four unshod horses, headed east, also. He spurred up on a rise just ahead, took out his old pair of Stouton binoculars and scanned the country. Red and brown hills, deep blue sky, the only vegetation cactus, sepa weed or bunch grass—-then, less than a mile ahead, riders came into view. Three: two men and a woman, it looked like, just coming up out of a small wash. Navajos. He could see the bows the men carried. The woman was riding an old white mare with a colt running beside it. Easy pickin'!! Three hundred dollars on the hoof right there.

And if the woman was young, maybe some fun first. He beckoned to his men, held up three fingers and grinned. The men all grinned back. Rifles were checked. The pace quickened.

The Redskins ahead didn't see them until they had covered more than half the distance between them. Then, one looked back and said something to the others and they kicked their horses into a gallop, the old mare rocking along with the colt right beside it. Fleck smiled, they were almost in range, just another couple hundred yards or so. But, to play with them a little, he eased up, letting his men come up, and they trotted along over the nearly level flat.

Up ahead, the men had fallen back, letting the woman on the old mare get ahead some. 'Poor fools thought they could protect her and them with just bows' he thought. Closer, closer.

Coming up was a low hill and the old white mare disappeared over it, the colt laboring to keep up with its ma. 'Be good eatin' Fleck thought.

It was his last thought. Suddenly, he was falling from his horse, the ground coming up and slamming him. He rolled and was dead when he stopped. Beside him, another man, Bones, came down in a splash of blood and brains, head shot. Now, the echo of rifle shots gave reason to the sudden dives of three men from their horses and the shriek of a hit horse, going to its knees. Harp was taking the bigger targets, as he'd been told.

The scalpers looked desperately for cover but there was none. Some fled back the way they had come. Those died first, because Ben and the others knew enough to get them before they got out of range. Some other men, braver, charged the guns. One got within a hundred yards before Harp took him from his saddle with a shot to the chest. Two men, their horses down, got behind them and tried to make it a rifle duel. They lasted the longest but were soon killed, both with head shots. Within less than three minutes, the scalpers were all dead and just the horses, minus two, were left on the field.

Jesho, Notsa and Bisti had pulled up behind the hill where the men's horses had been concealed and listened to the crescendo of firing with trepidation. How could four men kill twelve? Bisti urged them, "We should go home now. Maybe we can still get away."

Jesho considered.

"Not yet. Let me go see first. Then we can leave if we must." He dismounted and climbed up to peer over the top as the firing decreased, then stopped and turned back with a delighted grin on his face and waved them up.

140

They came and looked on an astonishing scene. Ben and the other men were walking down to the flat, their rifles held at the ready. The flat itself was cluttered with men and horses lying dead, and other horses standing with their heads down.

CHAPTER 21.

Black Mesa is a high long volcanic pressure ridge, covered with pinion and cedar, with pines rearing up at the top. In its foothills there are secluded small meadows and some seeps and springs. Generations of Navajos had intimate knowledge of the geography and over the years had congregated at points that would sustain greater numbers. Wolf Spring was one and there were nearly a hundred Navajos, mostly Yucca Fruit clan, gathered there for the Blessing Way chant that was to be done for Toi Keeyani, son of Pinto Keeyani, who was sickly.

Most were there who intended to come, so when a posted guard came with the news that there was a dust cloud headed their way, a bunch of horses and horsemen, Pinto gathered his warriors and made ready to fight, if necessary. Some were veterans who had fought the Army and hidden their weapons, mostly single shot rifles won from their enemy. Ammunition was scarce and few had more than several hoarded rounds. Most carried their bows. They spread out in strategic fighting spots, fingering their *Jish*,(medicine) praying to Monster Slayer or Born of Water, or some other of the Navajo deities.

Pinto watched as, out of the shimmering heat, a band of horses came walking in front of a small group of riders. As they came nearer, he saw that three were Navajo, and the others were *Bilaganna*, except that one was a huge black man riding an equally big horse. Packs were on some of the horses and now one of the Navajos came riding ahead. He was Nakleetsa Jesho. He waved. Pinto rose and waved back.

* * *

Pinto was a Navajo in his prime, of medium height, not overly large, but square and with an air of authority. Like most males of the tribe, he wore his hair shoulder length and banded about the head, a deerskin shirt with silver Mexican coins stitched on it, a sash for a belt that held up a breechclout and leggins that also had Mexican coins decorating the outside of the leg. He was a cordial host, especially when he heard what Jesho had to say regarding the recent demise of the scalpers. After they had eaten well at Pinto's hogan, his two wives serving them graciously under the spreading arbor, Notsa came out with the coffee she knew Ben and the others craved. She poured for them all and Ben lit a cigar that he handed around.

As Ben had predicted, the *Dineh* rejoiced that the band of scalpers had been wiped out. They were greeted with much respect and honor. The Indian scalps they had taken from the evil band were handled with veneration and properly buried under the direction of their most prominent medicine man, Hosteen Baatsolanii, who told the people how they must be handled. The horses were turned into the big herd and Brutus followed his buddy, Snake, which was just as well, since the Navajo's many dogs would have ganged up on him and likely killed him. He was just too foreign for them to easily accept right away. Ben had seen that there were a few good horses among the ones they had gained. He would let the three Navajos and the others all draw for them, too, when the time came to divide the spoils.

Then there was the guns and knives and other gear, camp stuff, and money belts. All would be divided seven ways, for the Navajos had risked their lives, also.

144

Meantime, he and his group were content to enjoy some eating and resting. He observed that Jesho and Notsa were doing much talking with their medicine man and Pinto. He supposed it was about them.

For his part, he enjoyed seeing how the Navajo did things. They were an old people that had a settled society. He could see that their lives had a pattern: they tended their flocks, moved them from desert to the high country, as the weather and grass warranted, had their particular food they ate, and had their religious beliefs—-a lot of them, if Notsa was to be believed. They had many superstitions: witches, ghosts, seers, magic, gods, spells, and more. They also had medicine men of different holy orders.

Ben, thinking back on it, remembered that Siccoolum had harbored many of the same beliefs. Were these common to all the various tribes? He thought they might be, but these Navajo certainly stood high as having the greater number. Every part of their everyday life seemed to be ruled by their religion. He was sure that he, as a white man, would never come to a complete understanding of it. The two worlds were too different. But he enjoyed the difference and the thinking of it.

* * *

Harp liked kids. And strangely enough, they liked him, after getting over his gigantic size and his blackness. He'd brought his little set of tools along from the boat and now he got them out of his duffel. Casting around for a suitable piece of wood, he found a mesquite root which seemed hard enough, and unrolled them. His little saw made a straight cut across the root at its widest part and the noise of the cutting attracted first one child, then a dozen, as he made another cut so that he had a nice chunk of malleable wood and began shaping it with his sharp carving knife and his chisels. Soon, he had a usable small bowl and he, after using his wood rasp, took a piece of sandstone and rubbed it smooth, then gave it to the first little girl who been watching him.

Delighted, she ran off to show it to her mother, while Harp was busy on something else from the remainder of the mesquite: a pony, which he worked on for just a few minutes, then handed it off to another child, this one a boy who took it to his father. In an hour, Harp had made a dozen items: spoons, bowls, ponies, men, bears, and more. He was working on a boat, there was a crowd looking on, and he was laughing as his big hands shaped the wood. The deep tones of his voice captivated the audience and when he started singing suddenly, they all sat down to listen. As Ben watched, the rest of the Navajos came drifting in and soon the whole clan was there, listening.

Will couldn't let Harp have all the glory, so he came over and they did some harmonizing together, working through their repertoire. Hank came and played his Jews harp with them and that instrument fascinated the Navajos further. Clearly, the men were enjoying themselves, too. Ben alone, stayed on the sidelines, but he enjoyed the singing, as usual. And as he sat there, watching, Notsa came and joined him.

CHAPTER 22.

They stayed through the winter and into spring. In that time, the Yucca Fruit clan's medicine man performed first the *Hochnchi Hatal,* the Enemy Way chant, a nine day sing to cleanse and shield the men who'd killed the scalpers of any evil spirits which might have followed them, seeking revenge. This the tribe did for free for them, in gratitude.

Then, two weeks later, after the first frost, the *Hozhoji Hatal,* the Blessing Way chant was performed. This was another nine day sing for Pinto's son, who had some unspecified ailment, possibly a bad heart, as he'd been born immature and was weak and sickly.

These two sings were exhausting to the clan, but enjoyable, too, as much celebrating and visiting was done. Ben noticed the absence of alcohol in any form, though there was some sort of bean eaten which seemed to cause the person to go into an emotional trance-like state. What it was, Ben didn't know, nor did he try any.

* * *

Any tribe that had horses liked a horse race, and the Navajo were no exception. With the coming of cooler days, some were held, usually at about a half mile, occasionally longer. Ben watched the first ones and did a little betting, after being invited to do so, by Pinto, Jesho or some other braves. The horses he bet on didn't win and he lost in succession, some sugar, some flour, some gold coins, and some bells and buckles. Hank had brought small folding knives, Barlows, and he won some bets or lost some, as did Will, who had brought scarves, ribbons and beads along.

Harp had his carved figurines to bet and he bet a lot, like the others, winning some and losing as many others.

Ben had been approached early by Pinto about trading for the scalpers' guns. These were a premium and almost a necessity if the Navajo were to protect themselves from other scalpers or renegades. Ben and Hank had inventoried their scalpers' arsenal: twelve rifles, mostly Winchester '73's or Henrys, but a couple Sharps carbines, 14 pistols, all Colts—big .44s, .36s and a couple hideout .32s. Knives of every description. Fry pans and kettles, utensils, horse tack, some flour, salt, sugar, etc., all things which were good trading stock.

The problem was, the Navajos wanted to trade sheep or goats or horses or blankets. They had little else to offer, except for some silver and gold jewelry.

The men would end up giving more than they got, unless a person factored in peace of mind.

* * *

The Enemy Chant had seemed to do them all some good. As Notsa had said would happen, at the end of the nine days, they had felt refreshed and cleansed, their minds at ease. But that wasn't the end of the matter: Will's leg was noticed and discussed and a hand trembler summoned, a *Ndiniihii*, Notsa called him. This medicine man was some kind of diagnoser of illnesses.

Through prayer, concentration and the use of some sacred pollen, the man's hand began trembling and he supposedly read Will's problem, which Will guessed was that much of it was in his mind, not just his bad knee, which the man wanted to see and touch. He said that Will needed a four day chant, the *Tzilhkichi Hatal*, the Mountain Chant, a long healing sing. At the end of it, Will proclaimed his leg—and his mind, better. Maybe he was, too, for Ben noticed he seemed more cheerful.

Hank's skin disease, all the freckles, was the source of much discussion, too, and it was proclaimed he needed a chant, also, the *Yoi Hatal,* the Bead Chant, which cured skin problems caused by thunder and lightning when a child. That, too, was held, but Ben didn't see that the sing diminished Hank's freckles.

Ben—-well, again more discussion was needed, with Notsa and some of the women thinking he needed a *Blessing Way* of his own and the medicine man sure he needed the *Klege Hatal*—the Night Chant. They compromised and opted for both, done a moon apart. Ben didn't mind so much. Sand paintings were an integral part of the sings and he was fascinated to watch how these were done so expertly, only to be wiped out that night, taking with them, Notsa said, the evil spirits they were supposed to attract. Both sings were long, involved lots of people as singers and dancers and artists, and all had to be fed while the sing was going on, to the expense of the one receiving the ceremony.

Ben and the others paid in good humor for the ceremonies—-in sheep, horses and other items. Despite the very pointed hints by all the Navajos, including Notsa, the men kept the guns to themselves, all of them. Ben had told them to do this for a reason: he wanted Pinto to come forward himself and propose the trade for the white children.

There were two, Ben had found, not just the one boy which Pinto owned. The other was a young girl and she was the property of Tohatin Keeyani, Pinto's old mother who was, Notsa said, notoriously hard to deal with, worse than Pinto himself. Well, they would see. Pinto wanted guns for his clan. Ben wanted the kids.

* * *

The last horse race was to take place that week. Then the horses would need to be left alone to get through the cold months. Ben laid back in the chair he'd built for himself and sipped his coffee in his new arbor, still interested in the ways of the tribe as the days sped past. He and the others were already resigned to the fact that they would spend the winter there. Oh well, it would be nice to be out of the northern blizzards, for a change.

Pinto had caused a hogan to be built for them, its doorway facing east as did all the others. It was a large one, to accommodate the other *Bilagannas* and *Yehtso-Bieth,* the giant black man. A ceremony was held which consecrated the structure, a one day sing only costing them one horse and some tack. They moved their accumulated gear in, the Navajos watching hungrily as they packed their rifles and other stuff into the fire-lit interior. Like all the hogans, the fire was at the center and all would lie with their feet to it at night. All their gear was packed in around the edge, by their heads. It was nice to have their own place.

The day before the horse race, Pinto and Notsa came to see him. Ben offered them coffee and a smoke and then they got to the point. Pinto had heard that Ben, whom they now called *Bezh-ntsah,* Big Iron man, wanted the *Nahtahn-Jakai-eshi,* the white corn boy, to take home to his family. Was that not so?

Ben waved casually, "Oh, tell him I have seen the boy and he is weak and small, not worth bringing back. He kin keep 'im."

She looked at him but translated. A look of concern passed fleetingly over Pinto's face. Navajo was passed back and forth, then Notsa said, "He asks if you will trade:

150

four guns, long ones, for the boy, with ammunition for them."

"Tell him the boy is not worth one gun. Tell him that I will bet one gun, a short one, against the boy on tomorrow's race. My pot-headed horse against any of his. Or two long guns for both white children."

More Navajo filled the air. "He says he will bet the two white childs against three long guns and ammunition for them—ten hands worth."

Ben nodded his head. "All right. We have a bet."

He reached out and shook hands. Pinto smiled, a grin that told Ben that he thought the guns were his. Ben smiled, too. Notsa looked from one to the other. She didn't smile.

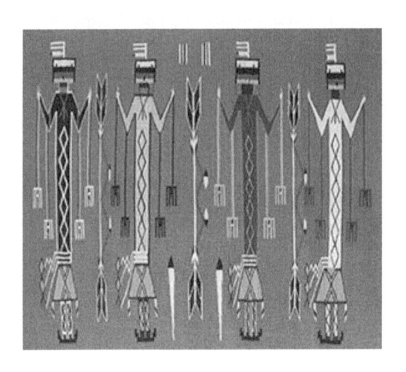

152

CHAPTER 23.

The field had seven horses in it. Ben saw that Notsa had Jesho riding her grulla, which according to Yaazi, had been his best horse, fast as the wind. Pinto had a beautiful bay that had proven fast, and there were three other Indian horses, two which looked good, one, a pinto, which was about as ugly as Snake in the head, but which was well put together and had run well in other races.

Ben had brought Snake in the night before and tied him to the front of the hogan, with Brutus in the doorway to guard him. He didn't think the Navajos would try any tricks, but who knew? Best to be safe.

The next day, after a mid-morning feast, the whole village repaired to the site of the races, marked off at about a half-mile, winding out to a large rock and back to the finish line. Pinto was insistent in walking the course with Ben, and Notsa and Jesho came, too. When they returned to the starting line, Pinto made a point of asking him if the course was okay. Ben agreed it was and the riders mounted. Right away, Ben could see that Snake was going to try some of his old tricks and was ready for him. The race would be won fair or not, with no cries of 'foul' over kicking and biting of the other horses.

A shout as the field came to the line, Snake a little behind, and they were off: with the grulla gaining the lead, the bay a close second. Snake shook his big head and thundered away, tied for third, maybe, it seemed to Ben.

153

In a bunch, they settled in and the horses stretched out. The rock came up fast and was rounded in a cloud of dust, the grulla falling back and the bay taking the lead, with the ugly pinto showing some surprising speed and passing Notsa's grulla to take a spot at second just past the rock. Snake circled the rock, slipped a little, regained his feet, and nearly unseated Ben with a lunging surge of speed that caught the grulla with a rush, then passed the pinto like it was trotting. Coming up on the bay, Snake charged to the front, Ben not even needing to quirt him, passing Pinto and winning by half a length at the finish. Behind them, came the bay, then the ugly pinto and the grulla. Ben turned and trotted back to an almost empty finish line.

"Where'd they all go? he asked Will and the others, standing there grinning.

"Hell, they all just took off for the camp. Poor losers, I guess. Or they don't want to pay up. We all bet on you. Good race, Ben!" The others echoed it.

Ben trotted Snake up to the hogan, got off and getting some sacking, rubbed him down and led him to water. Some of the other racers were there but no one spoke. Ben guessed that Indians couldn't stand to lose and ignored them, too.

* * *

That night, the tribe came to pay up and Ben treated them all with a cup of coffee and smokes, his last. Soon, the arbor was ringing with laughter. Notsa came and sat beside him and to his question, "What're they laughing at?" answered, "They laugh at the running pot-head horse you got. Yiee! How fast he is! How he passed them all with a swoop like an eagle flies. Now, Jesho is claiming his horse, my horse, was running backwards, that Bisti's pinto was running in mud, that Pinto's bay must have been hobbled. They all were tricked by the *Bilaganna's* ugly grundhzi, the horse that flies. Now, they say that they will

154

all pay their bets, but they will be destitute. They laugh at themselves. I laugh, too."

She smiled and Ben was dazzled by the show of white, even teeth in that lovely face. Losing to him hadn't seemed to upset her. Maybe they weren't poor losers.

He grinned, "Tell them that we, the other men and I, just wanted to teach them a little lesson. They can keep their bets. And we have some presents for them." He whistled.

At that, Harp, Will and Hank came in, each carrying the scalpers' rifles and pistols and began handing them out to the men, one to each, with later the ammunition to go with it. The men were astonished. Knives followed, then Ben came and made a special present to Pinto: a brand new Winchester '73 with an engraved receiver and a belt of cartridges. It was the one he'd bought for the trade for the boy. The man's eyes got wide. Ben compounded it by reaching behind him and coming up with the Stouton binoculars that the scalper leader had carried. These, he presented also to him.

"Tell him that we *Bilagannas* had our fun and now want to honor him and his people. Use the gifts for the good of the Navajo. May the *Dineh* walk in peace and harmony."

Notsa translated and the men were vociferous in their thanks, none more than Pinto, who seemed stunned. Notsa too, was confounded.

He says, "The children are yours. That you are all good *Bilagannas*." She grinned with delight.

"He also says that the *Hozhoji Hatal* sing must have guided your hearts to the right path. That they honor you."

She turned to him and took him by the hands. "I honor you, BenHite. You are truly the good man that Yaazi said you were." Then she ran from the hogan. That occasioned more Navajo and laughter. Ben busied himself

155

putting on more coffee, wondering if what he had seen in her eyes could be believed.

* * *

Ben greeted the two children, who had been washed and dressed in nice clothing. Though shy, Ben was able to work through that with the boy, who could still remember some English. In response to Ben's asking if he recalled his given name, he said,

"Yes, I know it. My name is Thomas Tackitt. My folks were John and Mary. I watched them die and promised myself that I would remember them and my older sister, Justine. I say their names every night in my prayers. The bad people threw them all in big holes after they killed them."

Ben felt pity and respect for the boy as he stood so straight before a stranger and spoke bravely without crying about losing his family. The little girl just stood sucking her thumb, wide eyed.

"You surely had a rough time, son. But we came here to bring you home to your grandfolks back in Harrison. Do you remember them?"

"Sort of. Gramma had white hair, I think. She was a good cook. She smelled good. I liked her cakes. Will she make me a cake when I get there?"

"Sure she will. I'll make sure to ask her, son."

"Can I say goodbye to Besana? She's crying. I hate to leave her."

"We won't be leaving right away and you can stay with her 'til we go, if you want. And I made up a present for you to give her."

He handed two bags of sugar and coffee to him to give to his Navajo family, who, it sounded like, were not happy to see him taking the children.

* * *

March winds were blowing across the desert and a smell of spring was in the air. It was coming on night and Ben was visiting with Pinto and Notsa under the arbor."I think another few days and we will be going north. We have been happy here, Hosteen Keeyani. We will hate to leave our *Dineh* friends."

Translating this seemed to upset Notsa and Pinto, too. "He says we don't want our friends to leave so soon, BenHite. Please stay longer."

"No, the waterholes are full now and the grass is growing on the trail. It's a good time to travel. Two more suns, then we pack and leave."

"It is a good time to travel, as you say, so we will pray for you to have a safe trip, my friend. Please come back to visit. Again, we thank you for what you did and what you have given us."

He rose and shook hands, something the Navajo didn't normally do, Ben had come to find out and he saw emotion in the dark eyes. He left and Notsa got up to go, too, a curiously forlorn figure.

"Would you stay a little, Notsa? How about another cup of coffee. Some's left in the pot." It was nearly the last of it, another reason to leave.

She poured and they sat, both a little uneasy, under the arbor. To their front, the two white children played with their friends in the dust, each sporting a horse and rider carved by Harp. Finally Ben said the words he had memorized. Years back, Siccoolum had told him that the best approach to an Indian woman was a direct one. He didn't know if that included Navajos, but he was going to find out this evening. Looking her in the eyes, he said, haltingly,

"Might it be that your heart rings like a bell with the sound of my name? Mine rings with your name— Notsa Begay— and I feel alone in my bed at night, wishing you were there. Will you come with me?"

157

Those lovely dark eyes widened. She was silent, looking out at the coming dusk, considering.

"Following your trail would mean leaving my people, Ben Hite, and that would be hard for me...but yes, if you would have me, I would come share your bed. But I would like to be married in the *Dineh* way. Later, if you like, we could have a Church Father bless us, also."

He gestured, and she came and sat beside him and he hugged her to him.

"Notsa, I was married before, and my wife, she was a good woman. Siccoolum was her name. But she got sick and died and I honor her memory yet. For long, there was no room in my heart for another. Now, with you, Little *Datatehe*, (hummingbird) there is."

Notsa replied, "It was much the same with me, Ben. I had a good man, but he was killed...by scalpers. Maybe even those you killed. I hope so." She looked down at her hands.

"My little girl was also killed. I was not there when they came. Often, I had wished that I was. Almost, I made it happen. " She looked up.

"But now, my *Bezh-ntsah*, I don't." A dark hand stole up and touched a curl behind his ear.

A day later, they were married in the Navajo way. The feasting and celebration took another two days before they were able to leave.

158

PART IV

Courtesy of the Library of Congress
Photographer: Edward Curtis

159

Virgin River Gorge

CHAPTER 24.

The trip back north was more difficult. The Colorado was up and they lost two horses and some food packs. Now, as they approached the Virgin River gorge, Hank came thundering from their back-trail and said, "We got company! A war party of twenty-five or so. Couple miles back. Comin' fast."

Ben looked ahead. "Right at this damn place! Almost as if they was tryin' to sweep us up in there. Wonder if they got a little surprise waitin' for us farther on. Well, let's go, but when we git in there, we'll stop at that little ridge we seen, remember, Will?"

He nodded. "Set up there?"

"Yeah. An' you two peel off just before then."

They went at a fast trot and soon came to the place Ben had mentioned: a large rocky bar which formed a cross-ridge that made a stopper in the canyon. They got off and tethered their horses fast, so they didn't spook at the coming gunfire. Hank and Will got their rifles and two shell belts apiece and each took an opposite side, going up side trails that would lead up and out of the high canyon walls. Once up on top there, they could place a dropping fire upon the attackers. But they would need time and that Ben and Harp would have to give them. Notsa had been receiving instructions on how to handle a rifle from Ben since the day after they had left Black Mesa and had proven to be an apt pupil, but she would have to stay with the children.

He had an extra Winchester carbine that he'd kept back from the gifting, a '73 .44 caliber that they had inherited from the scalpers. Now, she pulled it from the scabbard on her saddle, gathered the kids and, with Brutus, found a depression by the horses that offered some shelter. Above, a bright sun shone with a few high-flying clouds racing each other across the sky. Buzzards were sailing there as if they knew that a meal was forthcoming.

They didn't have long to wait.

* * *

A close packed group of riders—Ben thought, looking through his glasses, they were Kiowa—came at a gallop right up to the entrance of the gorge, where they pulled up, and a brave that Ben marked as the leader, got down and examined the tracks. Evidently, he saw they had all gone on into the canyon, for he swung up and with a gesture, they came on.

Ben centered his sights on that warrior and when they were well in the canyon, about 200 yards from them, he shot. The man fell, his horse skittering away from the body. At the same time, Harp pulled trigger and another brave went tumbling. The war party went to the ground and sought cover, a couple braves taking the horses back out of range, though Harp's second shot hit a horse.

Ben had fired three times—-all body hits, that with the big caliber, likely killed their man. Harp had gotten two shots off, both hits also. Now, warriors squirmed behind rocks or the dead horse and began returning fire. Now, bullets kicked up sand and rock chips at the ridge. It looked like a stand-off, when suddenly a shot echoed from the canyon wall on the left and a warrior half-rose, then toppled back. At almost the same instant, another shot came from the opposite side, killing another brave.

Yells of rage and fear came from those who remained and as Ben watched, the attackers began trying to fall back, amid a rain of shots from above. Ben chimed in, along with Harp, and the gorge rang with gunfire as the war party was shot to pieces. Very few made it out of the canyon alive, as Will and Hank both had a commanding perspective of the terrain below and kept up a barrage until there were no more targets. One last shot slammed that echoed from side to side and the gorge became still.

* * *

Hank had a good trail along the precipice above them and gestured that he would follow it, paralleling them as they went on deeper into the narrow passage. Will came limping down as they readied to start on, Ben having opened the pack on their steadiest horse, the big buckskin, and passed out more ammunition for their shell belts.

"Took care of that bunch!" he grated as he replenished his belt, too.

"Good shooting, Will, you and Hank hit them just as they were getting ready to rush us."

"Yeah. Don't think but three or four made it back to their horses. I doubt those'll come after us now. I want to go down and see what they had for guns, maybe pick up some ammo, too. We can always use it, if they have any of our calibers. C'mon, Harp."

He and Harp turned and walked warily down through the killing field, and scavenging quickly, shooting once when a wounded brave rose weakly to contest them taking his rifle from under his body, they gathered rifles and cartridges from the dead, each coming back with armloads.

Ben and Will sorted through it and kept out three good Winchesters that fired the same rounds as Notsa's— .44. There were two Sharps carbines and one Old Reliable'

163

long barrel which fired .45/70, which Ben, looking at, decided to keep, also.

They had the pack horses for them, having caught some loose horses, and they and the guns would be good trade stock, if and when they made it back to civilization. They wrapped them in some of the Navajo blankets, tied them securely, and fastened them into packs on the horses that they managed to catch from below. Ammunition went back in the ammo packs. The rest of the guns were hammered on the rocks until they were useless and tossed in the river. Ben hated to do that to good weapons and wished there had been some way to get them back to the Navajo.

* * *

An hour later, half way through, they heard firing. Ben halted them and scouted ahead, to see several Indians shooting up at what had to be Hank, who was lobbing rounds back with good effect. Ben eased forward and getting in a good position, began sniping, too. This caused a furor among the group, being set on from another direction, and they abandoned their positions, scurrying back, trying to get away. Hank kept up his bombardment and Ben shot until there were no more targets. The way was now clear.

* * *

As before, they scavenged arms and ammunition from the dead, destroying the guns not worth taking. "We got us a damn good bunch of rifles there. Worth a little money if we kin get 'im back. An' if we don't, at least they're out of the hands of those damn killers." Hank said as he saddled up again. "Some more horses, too. A couple pretty good ones."

164

The one being ridden by the Kiowa leader was a beautiful big sorrel that Ben had taken to, right away. As soon as he could, he wanted to try it out.

* * *

The Indians dispersed and the gorge traversed, they journeyed back on roughly the same trail they had coming down, reaching Parker's Ranch by the evening of the fourth day following the battle. Parker, was, as usual, a cordial host. He congratulated Ben on finding and retrieving the children, greeting them as he would a grown-up, to their confusion. Thomas solemnly shook hand with the grizzled rancher and the little girl gazed up at him with her thumb in her mouth.

Then his eyes bugged as the remainder of the pack train came in and he beheld the Indian horses loaded with blankets and guns. That all called for an explanation and Hank obliged him. Parker was tickled to hear that the Kiowa war party had been crushed, and surprised when he heard about the scalpers. He arranged a quick fiesta with Maria and her crew and they settled in for a short stay.

It soon became apparent that he wanted to do some trading for some guns and blankets and Ben handed that off to Will and Hank, being engaged in walking the kids around the new barn and helping Harp get the horses settled. Brutus, who was getting attached to Thomas, followed them. Parker's dogs, when they saw Brutus turn up again, had all lit out for cover, wanting nothing to do with the big pitbull.

The little girl, whom Notsa called Bei, tended to cling to Notsa, but had gone to Harp and Ben too, and all had taken turns carrying her on their horses. Ben put her on his shoulders and they made a circle of the stalls and visited Snake, Asa and Bill, Harp's Percherons, then had to go see Notsa's grulla, that she called Blue. Snake

165

wanted his usual little gift and Ben pulled some bread from his pocket and let Bei give it to him.

* * *

Parker had learned from the others that Ben had married Notsa and used that as an excuse to have a celebration. The fiesta started that night and continued into the next day and evening. On the fourth day, after resting, they began the journey back through Utah. The old Mex saddlemaker had made one for Notsa and Parker presented it to her. She rode it as they waved 'goodbye.' This time, Hank and Ben made sure that Will had a good supply to get him through the dry state, courtesy of Parker, who had traded a large amount of tequila and whiskey, along with some gold and silver from his secret trove, for the guns and ammo he wanted. Several horses stayed back in his corral, also, including the Kiowa sorrell, which he'd talked Ben out of at last.

CHAPTER 25.

Freddy was about to die, he thought, but he was damned if he would show yellow. Father Ben had taught him too well that a coward just keeps on running and the only way to respect oneself is to make a stand.

He and Lakey had come into the bar for just one quick one, then intended to go into the restaurant for a welcome meal. They were just getting into Fort Benton with the train and had finished unloading and taken care of their stock, then setting a guard on their wagons. The bar had been crowded and some of the men, they noticed, were trappers from upriver, who had come to town to sell their furs before the last of the boats headed downriver for the winter. Of particular notice was a tall one who kept a blue kerchief on his head, low down so it covered his forehead right down to his eyebrows. His gaze as it swept over them was chilling and both Lakey and he could feel something was up—tension was in the air. It came to a head when the man came over and with a French accent, asked if they were "Hite's men."

Lakey replied, trying to be gracious, "I'm his partner. This is his son, Fred Barnes. Have some business with us? Here, take a drink."

The trapper blinked, then snarled, "I'll tak more than a drink! The son of the man who did this to me is goin' pay with his own blood!"

He whipped off his kerchief and the man's forehead showed the scarred 'H' that Ben had inflicted on him. He began a move to the gun in his sash, the front sight snagged it momentarily and Freddy stood up, knocking his chair back at the same instant that he started his draw. Instinct had warned him and he had been ready for trouble when the man wove his drunken way over to their table.

Now, with a swift movement that became a blur, his pistol leapt into his hand and he fired twice: hitting the trapper once in the belly, once in his head, in the middle of the 'H' as he started down. Lakey moved, too, and his gun covered the other man's companions as they surged forward, coming from the bar to their friend's aid. They were too late, for he was dead when he reached the floor. They came to an abrupt stop and one, a thick bellied mustached old voyageur, said, "We try tell heem that he was too drunk to fight, but hees not listen!" He shrugged, gestured, and the trappers stooped and carried the dead man out the door.

Freddy and Lakey went to the porch and watched as they carried their dead friend down to the river bank, rifled through his pockets, took his moccasins and his sash, then dumped him in the river, where he floated away in the current. Behind them, a voice said,

"Excuse me, gentlemen, did they just throw that man in the river?" His voice was incredulous at the barbarity of such an act.

They turned and the talker introduced himself. He was a well-turned-out young gentleman in evening clothes right down to the gold headed cane, glossy pumps and the cravat. He held out his hand to Freddy.

"Elijah Turnbull, attorney-at-law. I saw your confrontation back there in the bar. You have a quick hand, sir. You are . . . ?"

Freddy and Lakey introduced themselves.

"May I buy you gentlemen a drink?"

168

They returned to the bar and found an empty table where they sat and watched amusedly as Turnbull went to the bar, rapped on it with his cane to get the bartender's attention and returned with their drinks. "Your continued health."

He drank his whiskey off with a practiced hand and watched as they both did likewise, then he asked,

"What caused the drunken fool to challenge you, Mr. Barnes?"

His query was one that normally a westerner would not consider asking. Too personal, too inquisitive for the frontier, whose populace knew enough to mind their own business or experience the consequences. But this man was a newcomer to the Territory. Freddy mentally debated the issue and decided he had no reason not to tell him. The young man had a likable air about him and a friendly countenance that invited one to confide in him.

"Well, the Frenchie had a run-in with my father. He's the one who carved that 'H' on his head. Guess the Frenchie decided he was going to take his revenge on me."

Turnbull considered that, rubbing the gold head of his cane. "I have trouble as an attorney grasping the fact that I have journeyed past the boundaries of Law and Justice. So. One man challenges another, is killed and no sheriff or police come to take the shooter into custody. Am I right in that assumption?"

"If you mean that I won't go to jail, you're right. He come and braced me in front of a room full of witnesses. Got what he had comin' to him."

Lakey nodded his assent.

"Been some talk of the govviment getting a U.S. Marshall up here but so far, none has showed up. This Territory is just too big and spread out for a couple men to handle. An' the Army has enough to give 'em fits, what with some of the tribes still warrin' with each other and ever' white they see. It's all wide open yet, from the

Canada Line down to Mexico. And if I was you, I'd start packin' a gun."

"Oh, but I do, sir." He reached in his vest and pulled a small Sharps derringer from it, showing it proudly.

Lakey snorted. "That little pea shooter! You shot somebody with that, about all you'd do is piss 'em off. Git off farther than a arm length and it's not accurate. An' two shots is all you got. What good is that when you got a bunch after you? My advice is to throw it in the river or stick it in yer boot, an' go get a real pistol."

He reached and pulled his Colt .45 single action revolver from its holster and handed it to Turnbull.

"Careful, she's loaded."

Turnbull grasped it gingerly, sighted at a picture of a nearly naked woman at the back of the bar, then, seeing some of the men over there in the direction he'd pointed showing some nervousness, handed it back hastily. Lakey, too, saw the bar's inhabitants getting a little agitated and stowed it away with a chuckle. Turnbull pulled on his drink.

"Well, seeing you men in action, I am convinced. I shall repair tomorrow to the mercantile and purchase one, together with a suitable means for carrying it."

"You goin' to wrap it around those clothes?" Freddy asked. "Pretty swell for way out here on the prairie."

"Well, I thought that evening attire after six was the proper protocol here in Fort Benton. Certainly it was in New York." He laughed quietly as he looked around. "I see I was wrong."

The conversation continued for a space, Lakey buying a last drink before they repaired to the restaurant together, Turnbull agreeing to eat with them. Freddy was starting to feel some after-effects of the shooting. Sweat popped out on him and he felt shaky. Food——he was suddenly not hungry. Lakey understood what was wrong and they excused themselves, saying they had to see to their livestock but that they'd be back.

The night was dark, with clouds over the moon as they walked down the street to the wagon park. They'd reached the gate when suddenly, from the dark beside the big livery building, came a silent group of men, knives in their hands. Freddy got his gun out just as two of them reached him. He shot twice. The assailant on his right grunted and went down. Then he was locked in a death struggle with the other, the knife coming in as he swung his Colt desperately and connected with the man's head. He slumped and Freddy thumbed the hammer back and shot him as he shook off the blow and started back up. The man went down and stayed.

Then Freddy turned to Lakey, who'd been swarmed over before he had time to draw his weapon. He lay on the ground, a dozen wounds in his body. Freddy saw dim shapes running and threw his last two rounds at them. One stumbled but kept on. Freddy went to Steele, trying to revive him, but his friend was dead, his throat cut and his blood running from other stab wounds. Freddy cursed, the adrenaline still coursing through his body. Reloading swiftly, he used a boot to turn his first man over. It was the thick bodied voyageur.

* * *

When dawn came, the Hite and Steele outfit were fully armed and primed for war. The eighteen drivers all packed their rifles and with Freddy at their head, they combed the town, finally rooting out three of the French voyageurs, one of whom was wounded in the leg. Pleas for mercy had no avail and they were hustled to a large cottonwood which stood near the river. There, one by one, they were strung up and left to dry in the sun. Their boss was buried in the Benton cemetery with most of the town attending the service.

Elijah Turnbull observed the procedure, shaking his narrow, neatly groomed head at the lawless vigilanteeism. Then he wended his way down to the wharf to buy a ticket on the first boat heading back to St. Louis. There was more business up here for morticians than there was for attorneys.

CHAPTER 26.

"I'd like to cash this, please."

The teller looked at the amount and his eyes widened. "I'll have to get the president to approve it, Ms. Barnes. Please wait a minute."

The elderly teller went into the office and shortly, the bank president came out, his pince nez perched on his slender nose. He held the check in his hand as if it were a snake.

"Do you really need such a ... large sum, Ms Barnes?"

"Yes. I do, sir, and I believe the check is in order. I would like it in twenties, please." Her cheeks were red with anger at the man's insufferable chauvinism. Men! The majority of them thought a woman wasn't capable of handling her own affairs.

The man sniffed and bit his lip, then went to the safe in his office and dialing rapidly, opened it and took out a bundle of money, from which he extracted bills. With an expert facility, he counted out five hundred dollars, put it into an envelope, and handed it to her.

"Please sign this receipt, Ms. Barnes and be very careful on the street with such a large sum."

"Thank you, you can be sure that I will." She put the envelope in her purse and marched out.

* * *

Katy was having man trouble again and getting damned sick of it. The brother to the man she had caused to be jailed had been showing up at odd times and places and threatening her with his stares and bold sneers. She'd finally had enough when her window was broken the night before, a large rock blasting through it. The police had arrived but had found no one. And a man couldn't be arrested on mere suspicion, so the sergeant had explained, projecting the same type of attitude that the bank president had just shown. It was likely just a boy's prank, he'd said. Well, <u>she</u> was going to do something about it. Father Ben had said that she should never hesitate, just use any means that worked to defend herself. And she would, by God.

After getting the money, that evening she went back to the school and with her key, opened it and went in. She rang a bell and presently a burly red headed man, the school's janitor, came down the stairs from his work on the upper hallway, a scrub brush in his big hand.

"You called, Miss?" He said with an Irish lilt.

"I did, Casey. I want to talk with you about a personal matter. Sorry to interrupt your work."

"That's all right, Miss. I was just after doin' the second floor hallway. Nurse Langstrom's new shoes leave black marks on the floor and they's hard to get off." He wondered what the beautiful young woman was doing here at this time of night, when she should be in her room, studying, or out with her beau.

"Casey, I heard that you were a professional fighter? Is that right?"

"Why...yes, Miss. Oi was. Beat 'Butcher' Bailey for the city championship in '74. Went 114 rounds with Angus 'The Bull' McWhirtle for the New York State belt in '76 but lost on a ....well, anyway, yes, Miss. To answer yer question. Had 38 fights. Won 34, two draws, two losses. But! They was not me fault." He held up his right hand, the knuckles of which were flattened and ridged with scar tissue and bone.

"Broke me hand the once and then was sick wit the flux the other time, an' that weak. Couldn't come to the scratch that night after 25 rounds."

She listened with interest, more certain than ever that this was her man.

"So. If I was to ask you to thrash a man for me, so that he would leave me alone, you might consider it?" Her eyes flashed and the man thought once again that she was as beautiful a young woman as he'd ever seen.

"If any scrub was to bother yez, I would take it an honor to punch his lights out fer him, fer nuttin'." He curled his massive fists at the thought.

"I have been bothered, but I want to pay you, Casey. This is strictly business and I don't want to be obligated to you. (or any man, she thought) How much?"

"Well...if it's business, now, a hundred dollars should do it. Half now. Half after the job is done."

"Here is the fifty, then." She counted out fifty dollars. (Cheaper than I thought) "I will give you the other fifty when it's done." She looked at him.

"Don't break any bones but do a good job. And tell him to leave me alone or the next time, you won't be so gentle."

He folded the bills into his shirt pocket and smiled. "Whut's this cove's name, Miss?"

"The brother of the man I shot, Raymond Tomkins. Albert Tomkins. I don't know where he lives. He's from up-state, as they say. I've seen him go into the Second Street Saloon. I think you might find him there or maybe they know where he is."

* * *

The next day, Casey entered the Second Street Saloon & Billiards on his noon break and inquired of the

175

bartender if there was a man there named Albert Tomkins. He was supposed to deliver a package to him. The bartender barely looked up from his paper.

"Yeah, that's him over there playing pool. The one with the cigar in his mouth."

Casey walked over to the player, seeing a young man, tall, with an arrogant look about him. His clothes made him out to be somewhat of a dandy. His being in the saloon instead of on the job somewhere made him either well off or just plain lazy. Casey, who'd worked nearly every day of his life, decided that this job might have some pleasure to it.

He stood by the table until the two men playing noticed him, then with a diffident air, said, "Oi was supposed to deliver a package to Albert Tomkins. You'd be him?"

"Yeah, Mick, I'm your man. <u>Mr.</u> Albert Tomkins. Who's the package from? Where is it?"

"Oi didn't git the name. It's in me cart. Kind of heavy. Could yez help me unload it?"

"I guess I could. Huh. Wonder what it is?"

He followed Casey out the door and on the step, said, "Where's your ca...." That was as far as he got.

Casey grabbed him and threw him into the alley, and laying him out with a tremendous right that surely meant a black eye, said, "There's yer package. From Ms. Katherine Barnes, who kindly asks that you quit botherin' her. Or, she says, the next time, Oi'm not to be so gentle."

Then he picked the dazed fellow up and delivered another blow to his middle, making him spew his beer and kittles. Five minutes later, dusting his hands with a job well done, Casey walked out of the alley with a whistle on his lips. He thought it might be the easiest hundred dollars he'd ever made. And on his lunch break!

* * *

176

"I'm delighted to see you deposited most of the money you withdrew, Ms. Barnes. Very thrifty of you. 'Waste not, want not,' you know. I hope you got good value from your expenditure."

"Yes, it _was_ money well spent." Casey had assured her that the gentleman would be eating his food lying down for awhile, if he could get any in his mouth.

'The nosy bastard. If he knew what I had spent the money on, he'd likely faint dead away,' she thought scornfully as she exited the bank.

CHAPTER 27.

Waterwheel was being honored with a new name. It was often customary in the Plains tribes to replace the early name of the youngster with one that better reflected some exploit or medicine dream that he'd had. His old name, Whaddawheala, (Little Badger) would be thrown away and his new one, Es-Kah-Teh-Mes, (Kills The Man twice) presented at a feast given in his honor by Takes The Enemy's Gun, his adoptive father and mentor. Takes The Enemy's Gun was of the Burnt Mouth clan and so most of the braves invited to the feast were of that clan, including Many Coups, the chief.

Though buffalo were getting scarce, a fat cow had been killed by Takes The Enemy's Gun and after sharing with others of the tribe not so fortunate, he had kept the loins back for the naming ceremony. After an hour, they were replete with the savory meat and the vegetable stew made by his wife. Now, Swift Deer took up his drum and started into a lively rhythmic tom-tomming that finally crescendoed to a thunder, then died back to a closing soft tapping.

Takes The Enemy's Gun got up and offered his pipe to the four directions, then lit it and taking a few puffs, started it on its way around the lodge, passing it as the sun goes, from east to west. Each man took it as it came to him, offering it first to the Sun, the Father, then to the

Earth, the Mother of all things. When the pipe was smoked out twice, Takes His Enemy's Gun said,

"We know of the medicine dream that our chief, Many Coups, had in his childhood, when it was foretold that the buffalo would disappear from the earth and the White men's spotted cattle would take their place, that the White men would defeat the tribes that fought against them and take their lands. The dream also told the Absarokee that they were foolish to fight against the White men, that we must prove our friendship by fighting with them against the other tribes. This we have done, even to helping their Army chiefs by acting as wolves when we were needed.

Now this has all come to pass, and the White man has defeated the tribes but their young men still sometimes come in war parties against us, seeking our scalps, our women and our horses. Thus we still need to be watchful that our enemies do not leave us on foot, whining like dogs as we watch them carry off our women.

So, to keep our hearts strong, we ourselves go on the war trail against them, for how else can our young men count coup, gain the respect of the older warriors and by bringing back horses, get wealth to pay for the women who enter their hearts?"

The lodge resounded with the "Waugh, Waugh" of agreeing warriors, the drum kept up its soft tapping and Takes His Enemy's Gun went on,

"I went with Many Coups on his last war trail and took with me my new son, Little Badger, to be a pup to our wolves, for it was his first time. This young man comes from the home of Faraway Gun, a white warrior whom you have heard myself and Many Coups speak, and listened as I told how, on our war trail against the Blackfeet, the white man saved my life twice. Therefore when his son came to me and asked for shelter in my tipi, and wanted to become a Crow, I was honored to have him by my fire. We became close as the fingers in a fist and I decided to adopt him into my lodge and the tribe. Always, he had wanted to fight with us against our enemies, for his heart is strong, strong as his father's!

Thus, we went against the Sioux to see if we might steal back some of our horses they had taken in the moon of Falling leaves. And of course, to spill some of their blood, if we could. Altogether, we were fifteen, and we went fast, making it to the Greasy Grass stream where we found a big village and seeing their horse herd, decided to teach them a lesson by taking them all.

Many Coups sent some of us wolves to the far side of the village to shoot and decoy their men off that way while the rest killed the herders and drove off the herd, which was many horses.

We wolves who went to the other side of the village were given some time to work our way into the circle and try to steal some of their war horses, and Little Badger followed me as we covered ourselves with buffalo robes and crept forward until we saw a chestnut horse tied before a large tipi. I told him that I would go cut that one's rope, to watch for me while I did. As I was cutting it loose, it snorted and its owner poked his head out of the door of the lodge. Little Badger shot him and he fell back in. Then I cut the horse loose and jumped on its back. As I did so, the man came back out and shot at me. Little Badger rushed forward and took his gun from him and hit him with it, then shot him again. That time, he scalped him.

Then he jumped up behind me and we, both shooting as we went, circled our side of the village. Aiiee! That was a ride! Now the Sioux were up and rushing to us, trying to kill us. Three times, men came out of their tipis and shot at us, but the chestnut was fleet and we finally ran right though the village, where there was much shooting and shouting, and there Little Badger did another brave thing——he jumped off and with his empty rifle, struck a Sioux just climbing on his horse, a big pinto. The man fell and Little Badger leaped on it and came with me.

181

Though many shots were fired at us, none hit us or the horses and we got away from the camp. Soon, we caught up to the herd and helped them get away, though to do so, we had several times to fall back and fight, for not all the horses had been taken and some of the Sioux caught up to us.

In those fights, Little Badger showed that his father, Faraway Gun, had taught him well, for he could shoot farther than we could and hit more often. Soon they grew afraid of us and we were left alone, to come home with the Sioux horses. Though that was Little Badger's first war-party, he showed us all that his heart is strong, that his aim is straight and his courage steady. Therefore, I give him his new name, Es-Kah-Teh-Mes, <u>Kills The Man Twice</u>!

The lodge resounded, with all the warriors calling out the new name, the drum reaching a new crescendo and Whaddawheala was no more. Kills The Man Twice was now a full fledged Crow Warrior of the Fox Society.

CHAPTER 28.

Although no reservation had yet been established for the Crow, an agency headquarters had been. This establishment took the form of a crude log fort, a hundred feet square, with a cannon mounted on the most strategic side. The agent, a regular army officer named Major Camp, treated with the Crow there and to cultivate better relations, employed several trustworthy white men or half-breeds who could speak both English and Crow. These men had various duties: watchmen, dispatch riders, interpreters, wood choppers, carpenters, blacksmiths and teamsters, and so on. Their most important job, though, was to promote friendly relations between the two races.

There was also a store, owned by Nelson Story and run by John Waddell, an Englishman, which was used by the tribe, where white goods and food could be bought. (at a tremendous mark-up) Furs and robes were the normal trade items used by the Crow, though horses and meat sometimes were, also.

Blankets, beads, sugar, flour and coffee were commonly sought by the squaws, along with cloth and metal pots and pans. Powder, primers and lead were needed by the braves, as most still made do with black powder weapons. The lucky few, though, were in possession of the new cartridge guns, the best of them being the Henrys or the newer Winchesters. These were coveted by all the warriors, as their enemies seemed to always be better armed than they were.

Kills The Man Twice was already well armed when he came to the Crow, with the Winchester .44 and a Colt .44 pistol that Ben had given him when he left. Ammunition was obtainable at the post and he had money, so had purchased a good quantity, along with a used Henry, that he gave to Takes The Enemy's Gun when he asked to join the tribe.

The fact that he was well armed and rich in horses, combined with the fact that he could speak good English, brought him to the attention of Major Camp and he offered him a position working for the Agency at fifty dollars a month. His duties were quasi-law enforcement, as Camp gave him a badge he'd had made in Bozeman that said, "Agency Police".

"What you're to do is help guard the horse and cattle herds, along with LaFarge, the one they call "Horse Rider" and some others. Many Coups is the boss. Take his orders. Do your best. We're constantly losing stock."

To wean the Indians off of the buffalo, which were fast disappearing, anyway, the government had authorized Camp to purchase livestock. This he did, as the occasion arose, buying worn-out oxen or other beef cattle that had made it up to the gold camps, and letting them graze on the rich grass along the rivers until such time as they would be butchered.

As more and more white men came into the country, though, stock thieving grew to be a business. Since many men arriving were former Confederates who hated the Union blue anyway, the idea of stealing from the federal government AND the Indians, too, was an attractive and tempting objective. Then, too, the other tribes continuously had to be dealt with, though they were mainly after horses and scalps. Accordingly, Camp had been vigorous in enlisting the bravest and best of the Crow to keep the livestock and the agency safe. At their head, rode Many Coups, their chief.

* * *

After nearly a year, Kills The Man Twice was happily ensconced in the bosom of the Crow tribe, just where he wanted to be, not living as a white man like his mother had. He'd loved her and honored and respected Ben Hite, but he was an Indian and this was where he knew he was supposed to be.

Here, he had found the life he'd dreamed of: riding his horses, hunting, the company of others of his skin color, and sometimes, the danger and adventure.

Several times now, they had chased horse thieves. It was usually Piegan, who were like magpies—seemingly always around. The northern Indians usually came on foot, seeking horses. The Sioux and Cheyennes usually came on horseback, seeking scalps, women, then horses.

Once, Many Coups and his men had trailed a bunch of Piegan who had taken a dozen horses, to the river, where they had crossed with them, then waited in ambush until the Crow had begun fording and started shooting. A brave named Yellow Horse had been killed. That had turned the Crow back and they had camped and waited until night, then crossed and followed hard on the trail. The Crow warriors had the better horses and the Piegan had finally forted up on a butte overlooking the Musselshell.

There the Crow had surrounded them and kept up the siege until that night, when the Piegan had slipped away and escaped on foot. All that were left were a of couple blood spots and the horses, which had been ridden hard. Many Coups said then that the Piegan were as slippery as snakes and maybe the best horse thieves of all the tribes. The Agency was always losing horses,

185

sometimes from right close to the fort, and most times they were trailed going off to the north, crossing the river, which meant either Piegan or Flathead.

Another time, he and Takes the Enemy's Gun had been detailed to follow twenty head of beef stolen by what Many Coups had determined were two white men, heading south. Many Coups had cautioned them against killing them, if they could help it. White thieves were supposed to be captured and turned over to the Army but that time, when they had caught up to the rustlers, they had made a fight of it. Takes The Enemy's Gun killed one, and Kills the Man Twice shot the other.

Both were dead and they left them where they lay, taking the horses and the guns. Nothing was said, though Camp heard of what had occurred, and Many Coups shook his head sadly at their report. Both men decided that they couldn't have done anything else and that maybe it would send a message to those who thought that the Agency beef was easy to steal.

* * *

Lately, Takes His Enemy's Gun's wife, Nootoh (rabbit) had been making some pretty obvious hints about their adopted son taking a wife for himself and setting up housekeeping. A number of girls seemed interested in him and he was having trouble making up his mind. One in particular, a tall, willowy girl who seemed always to be laughing, was more and more in his thoughts. Her name was Seetaka, (Antelope) and he thought he detected a liking for him in her flashing eyes. Nootah said she was a hard worker.

This would clearly take some more thought.

186

CHAPTER 29.

"Now, Brigham, You know that I know Haight and Lee and the others in the Iron County Brigade was just doin' what you said was fine and right to do—-kill Gentiles and take their belongin's off their dead bodies. Why, we got 'em goin' to California and them thet's comin's back with their pockets full. The Lord only knows how many's a'lying in unmarked graves out there." Rockwell winked. The beady deepset eyes twinkled.

"An' He ain't tellin'. The Tabernacle itself was built on such funds, I s'pect."

He took a chew from his pocket, looked at it, and ripped off a hunk, then offered it to Brigham Young, who looked at it distastefully and shook his head. "Uncle Port" as he was called by the Mormons, went on, as Brigham knew the acid tongued old killer would. He put up with him because he really did know where all the bodies were buried. Most of them, he'd killed. Unfortunately, he was getting old.

"An' now you had yer boys shot up tryin' to take the Hite outfit, got the U.S. Army all hot an' bothered, with letters from the President hisself comin' in, threatening to make you step down as Governor of this fine state, an' you hev to call on old Porter to cover yer ass fer ye."

187

Porter Rockwell, the leader of the Danites, the Mormon's chief 'Avenging Angel,' a man attributed to a hundred deaths and more in the Zionist cause, a killer whose tally exceeded the total of Wyatt Earp, Doc Holladay, Wes Hardin and Billy the Kid, had finally been sent for by the Mormon Prophet.

No longer a viable threat, as his youth was gone and his health was bad, yet he still was a formidable man, with eyes that pierced through and through, and massive hands. Unfortunately for the Mormons, those eyes were dim now with cataracts and the hands had a tremble to them.

"I didn't ask you here to flay me with that poison tongue of yours, Port. Just to have you tell me who I might turn to that could do a quiet job of work for me, such as you used to do so well."

"Oh, I figured you had that in mind, Brigham. So, I brought him along. He's waitin' outside while we settle the...details, so to speak."

"What I want is satisfaction. Ben Hite and his Sharpshooters killed eighteen of our Brothers and stole my children. I got them back but had to pay plenty. I want them dead! 'Revenge is sweet,' the Bible says."

"I heard that. Yes, I did. Eighteen men and yore kids gone. He damn sure put you over a barrel, yessir!" Though they were religion bound, brothers in Mormonism, it didn't mean they had to like each other. And it made Rockwell chuckle to know Young's nuts were in a vice.

"Port, It's worth ten thousand to me to have his head brought in. Another five thousand for each of his men. I hear now that there were only him and his two friends. Three men, Porter! If I had known there were so few, I'd have gone after them earlier."

"Three damn good men, Brigham. Expert riflemen against a bunch of sod-kickers, coopers and carpenters. Men who could knock the eye out of a deer at three hundred yards. Not ordinary men. And they'll cost ye extra. Ten thousand apiece. And five fer expenses. It'll cost fer some men and some travel."

Brigham glared but his gaze was locked in a stare-down with a man who could barely see, his form a dimness in the office light. He grunted and gave in.

"All right, dammit! Ten thousand. When I see their heads. The expenses I can do right now." He pulled a drawer open and took some bills from it, handed them over with a sour look. Rockwell tucked it away.

"Tsh, tsh, Brigham, I know where that money's comin' from, and it ain't from yer pocket. 'Sides, think of the satisfaction ye'll have, seein' them heads."

He went to the door and beckoned, "Come on in, Hoyt, an' meet the Govvinor hisself. He wants ye to do a job fer 'im."

* * *

Later, back at Porter's cabin, the two men made their plans. Porter would gather some others of his cronies and provide the horses. Hoyt Drake would need at least five more 'helpers.' But they would be paid good day wages only—ten dollars and found.

"An' the best men ye kin find with a rifle, Port."

"Why, Hoyt, the best way to kill a man is to catch 'im when he's not lookin'. The black of night always worked fer me. An' it don't matter how good he is, if you shoot first 'er put the knife in real deep."

There was the final difference between Rockwell and the rest of the West's trigger men. Some of them might have killed men from ambush, but seldom did they work at night. Rockwell, on the other hand, did almost all of his killing after nightfall. By day, as Sir Richard Burton, who had met him on his trip west had said, he was a genial old assassin with a wit about him who liked a drink and a story.

189

He had for years been The Prophet's doer of special works. Those works included backslid Mormons who needed to be brought back in the fold. But there had been a time when he had been sent to California to graze on the easy pickings there and send back money for the Cause. It cost heavily to wrest a Garden of Eden out of prairie and desert, and Porter had helped mightily in the financing end.

Now, with his strength and eyes gone, he had given over his special work to Hoyt Drake, a young Mormon who had idolized Rockwell and wormed his way into his confidence. So far, the man had proven, while not as adept as Porter in his younger years, certainly as fanatical in the Cause of the LDS Church. Both were a strange mixture of devout religionists and merciless killers, just two of several the Mormons had spawned after their hard early times of persecution by anti-Mormons in the east. Drake had been one of the men who had besieged the Perkins train and participated in the killings. He had been elsewhere on assignment though, when the Iron County Brigade had gone after the Hite wagons.

* * *

The Gold Rush and the Civil War had been times of great opportunity for the Mormons. They were in dire need of funds. And here came the purse carriers, right into their web of evil, delivering up their money. During the War, the government had no time for either Indian depredations or the Mormon problem. After the terrible conflict though, the federal government had finally gotten fed up with the continued reports of Gentiles being abused, robbed and killed as they attempted to pass through Utah to or from California and Oregon, culminating in the incident of the Mountain Meadow Massacre. A new governor and miscellaneous federal appointees to the territory of Utah had been sent out to take Young's place.

He was, of course, rejected by the Mormons, for the whole state of Utah was firmly in the hands of the religionists by then. He was sent back east in disgrace and General Albert Sidney Johnston had therefore been commanded by President Buchanan to quell the "Mormon Rebellion" prompting Brigham Young who had called it an invasion, to issue a proclamation of war.

Drake had been with Rockwell when his Danites had participated in the guerrilla action which had been successful in denying the mountain passes from the approaching army, bottling them up on the desert. Then, they had captured three large Army supply trains carrying 500,000 pounds of provisions intended for the Army column's maintenance during the winter.

The Danites set fire to the trains, then went on and burned Fort Supply and Fort Bridger, two depots with other caches of supplies, thus denying the Army further. The Army's cattle herds were driven off and eventually the Army was reduced to eating its horses and begging food from the very people they had come to conquer. Johnston was finally forced to retreat with his tail between his legs, which delighted the Mormons and had made a hero of Rockwell and his 'Avenging Angels'. People as far away as Europe flocked to the Mormon Cause.

* * *

When Rockwell had returned to Salt Lake City, he and Drake had been given state marshal badges and ordered to escort six prisoners back to California. These men had originally come from California to open a gambling hall and houses of prostitution there in Salt Lake but had been arrested when their attentions became known. Young had decreed that these 'fomenters' be deported back to California and Rockwell and his men given the chore. The men were escorted out of town and disappeared.

191

Later, bones were found and by some means, the bodies were identified as the six who had disappeared. This was known as the 'Aiken' case, named for the two brothers, John and Thomas Aiken, and achieved some notoriety in the press later. However, nothing was done about it, as no one wanted to prosecute. And the six were by no means the first or the last to fall into Rockwell's clutches by way of Mormon law and die, usually resisting arrest or trying to escape.

But few of Rockwell and Drake's deeds were so easily uncovered. It was whispered that there was a deep unused well on Rockwell property that was filled nearly to the top by bodies. Of course, his property was off-limits to Gentiles.

And now, Drake was appointed to carry out the operation against the Sharpshooters.

* * *

They sent for five of the top Danites: Tom Algren, a blonde bearded young Viking who habitually packed his Sharps .50 rifle and was considered a dead shot, Ed Beck, an older silent Indian fighter who had become a legend after Utes had killed his family and he had begun a vendetta against them that still continued, with upwards of twenty-five kills to his name. Vincent Pitt was a sidekick of Drake's who practiced a sadistic bent toward his victims, and liked to hear them scream. Jake Wattley, was a Danite of Rockwell's crew whose prowess with rifle and pistol was respected by the other 'Angels.' Lastly, Lot Collins, a man of respected ability with rifle and pistol, but especially with a knife, who had over twenty kills himself to his credit. Like Rockwell, he liked the night.

It had been Algren's, Pitt's and Wattley's shooting that had caused the Perkins train to finally surrender, after seven of their bravest men had been killed by long range sniping while trying to reach water for their families.

These three, with Drake, had also been in on the final massacre of the defenseless train members, when they surrendered their arms and began their death march into the waiting arms of the Paiutes and the Mormon killers.

Young's intricate web of intelligence throughout Utah had uncovered the possibility of Hite being a member of a party who had headed south the year before. The villages and stops along the routes had all been alerted of the possibility that they might come through again, headed back north. Now, they'd been sighted in Provo, headed up the Provo River to cross over to the Sienna. Scouts had dogged them and passed the information along to Young, who had given it to Rockwell. That night, he shared the particulars with the assembled group.

"Four men, one a big black, a squaw and a couple kids. One a' the men is supposed to be Ben Hite, the leader of the Sharpshooters. Likely, the other white men were with him when he killed our brethren over on the Ogden trail. Don't know anythin' about the darky. He's likely just a servant. We know Hite had a squaw with him when he lived by Ogden. Probably the same one. The kids, who knows. They're all fair game and when you git any of 'em in yer sights, go ahead an' kill 'em. We're payin' ten dollars a day and found and head money of a thousand fer Hite, seven hundred fer each of the two white men and two hundred fer the rest. Suit ye?" It did. Since they'd heard the men were likely the Sharpshooters, who had killed friends and Church members, they'd have gone after them for nothing.

"Catch 'em by surprise when they come out of the canyon there and ye shouldn't have any trouble settlin' their hash fer 'em. Was I you, ye might try a night sneak if ye git a chanct. Kill 'em in their beds." He grinned. It was the grimace of a snarling wolf.

"One thing. To git yer head money, we'll want the heads. I like to take a little salt along to dress 'em down with. Makes 'em stink a little less."

193

The men all agreed that made some sense, most having experience in that regard.

Orrin Porter Rockwell
Image courtesy of Wikipedia

CHAPTER 30.

As they came closer to the Mormon center, Ben grew more uneasy. He had the sense that they were being followed and catching glimpses of men trying to keep concealed heightened the tension. Talking with the others, he found they had the same feeling: that they were walking into a trap but could only continue their regimen: scout ahead and be alert, keep their weapons to hand and be ready to use them. He also resisted the urge to hurry the horses. They needed their daily graze and water. So, the party wended its way north through the east side of the Wasatchs even more cautiously then they had gone south.

The trail was clear so far, though they encountered several small parties of travelers on their way that were as wary of them as they were, keeping a distance and yelling to each other as they described the track they had just traveled over. The Mormons had a reputation now that made all Gentile travelers cautious.

The night before they were to exit the mountains and wind through a narrow passage way, which Ben wanted to traverse in the daytime, they stopped early at a small stream and made their evening camp. Ben decided to detail Harp for the late night's guard and took him aside.

"Harp, I just feel that we're goin' to be hit, likely a night attack, since they're shy of our shootin' during the daytime. That means they'll try to pull a sneak on us, and you being the right color, you can move in the dark better than any of us 'whiteys.'" They both grinned. Facts were facts.

"Here's a blanket thet'll keep you warm but I'd go without a shirt. Can't see you, then, if you don' smile." He handed him the darkest blanket they had, and Harp said,

"Razor time, Boss." He drew his big razor out of his pants and flipped it open.

"That's right. And I'll be out there, too, so don't cut on me and I'll try to do the same fer you."

The night came down early in the mountains and soon it was pitch dark, with clouds obscuring the sliver of moon, which was in its quarter phase. Harp went out to the east a hundred yards and set up the way Ben had taught him: hunkered down so that the horizon was visible and he could see any variation that might appear. With the blanket covering him, he was warm and nearly invisible. He'd rubbed himself with sage, so any odor would be masked. He kept his razor in his hand and his holstered Colt ready. His rifle, he left on his saddle. Any action in the night would be close quarters. And now, it was time for patience. He made his mind blank and trusted to his senses.

Ben, across from him, did much the same. He also had a blanket that covered him and with his knife in his hand, felt focussed in his mind. He had made the others make up formed beds and sleep away from the fire. They, too, were keeping their weapons handy.

* * *

Pitt and Collins were waiting for night, then the others around the fire would back up the two men by surrounding the party from aways back, and waiting until they had crept into position. If the guard was not alert and they could take him out without alerting the rest of the

196

party, then maybe some more throats could be slit. They'd move in when the moon went down.

Harp was strung tight as a wire when the horizon changed imperceptibly over on the right. *Something* was coming close. He squinched his eyes and saw, dimly outlined, a man on his hands and knees. He waited and the man came on, crawling slow. Harp sprang and flattened the figure, slashing with his razor in a quick, flicking motion. The man squealed under the black man's weight and tried to stab backwards in an awkward fashion. Harp grabbed the man's face with his left and pulling it up though the man tried to fight him, brought the straight razor across and slashed his throat, stroking it twice. The blood gushed. Harp rolled off him and looked around, alertly. The night was quiet, then, from across the fire, he heard a muffled cry.

* * *

Ben had glimpsed the man as he came past him. He jumped then and the blanket caught his leg, slowing him just a trifle. The man turned and his knife came up, catching Ben's arm as he landed on him. Ben came around with a fist and caught the man a hard lick in the face, which diverted his attention for an instant. Then Ben's knife was into the man's chest, causing him to cry out. Ben hit him again and then struck once more with his blade and the man slumped, but not before he had stabbed Ben in the leg. Ben, upset because he'd botched the job and gotten himself hurt, stabbed the man one more time.

Trying to watch the horizon, he cut the man's shirt off him, noting that he was a big individual, then used some of the tail to staunch the flow coming from his leg. The sleeves went to tie around it, holding it on. It was the leg that worried him, the same leg that had been broken during the stable fire. It was hard to tell in the dark, but he

197

didn't think any arteries had been severed, however. The blood was flowing, not gushing out.

The upper arm was ripped, but the sleeve had caught some of it, and he wrapped his kerchief around it and forgot it for now. It would be dawn soon and he'd have Notsa take care of it, then. He was worried about Harp, but they had both to stay where they were at until daylight. Now, as he sat beside the dead body, the night was quiet. His wounds burned.

* * *

The sun came up late over the mountain rims. Ben was stiffened with the hours of sitting in the cold and his leg buckled when he warily moved in to the burned out fire. Hank and Will saw he was hurt and came to him. Harp was still out on guard. Soon, Notsa appeared with the children. She ran when she saw him lying there and while they were attending to his wounds, Ben said,

"Hank, there's got to be some still out there. You and Will better go take a look. Take 'em if you can. Notsa will do fer me."

The two men turned without a word and melted into the dim, dawn light. They met Harp coming in and he told them he had glimpsed a man moving away from a position out several hundred yards just before. They continued on away from the group and soon separated, sneaking as only experienced war veterans and sharpshooters can. They were in time to see men riding away, leading two riderless horses. Will whipped out his glasses and steadying himself, sighted four men, riding hard. They were looking back, expecting shots, but were already nearly out of range.

"Try a shot, you think?" Hank asked, sitting down and running his sight up.

"I make it 700 yards, and they're moving fast. Up to you."

198

Hank replied with a stroke of his trigger, sending a bullet downrange that, Will, watching through the glasses, saw made a horse stagger and go down. Instantly, Hank had another on the way. Will never saw where that one went, then they were over a hill and out of sight.

"Knocked a horse down with the first. Couldn't see what the second did." Will told him.

Hank grunted. They turned and went on back.

Notsa and Harp had cleaned the ugly stab in the leg, which luckily hadn't hit an artery. It was deep and had bled clean. Notsa had torn one of her skirts for bandages and compresses and made good use of them. The arm injury was a four inch gash and Notsa pushed the edges together and wrapped it tightly after treating it, too, with *Doctor Alstetter's Remedy,* brought along by Ben. He swore by it for wound treatment, having used it for his horses and other hurts to both animals and men. From the smell, there was a high amount of alcohol in the mixture. Will had wanted to try it as a drink, but Ben had sternly denied him access to it. Now, they were glad that Will had not consumed it.

"Can you ride?" Hank asked when they got back. "We need to be moving on, 'er they'll be back with some more men."

Ben struggled up, "I got a choice? Help me git on. We'll chew on jerky down the trail."

They got him into the saddle and were soon on the move. Will had stayed back a ways, Hank rode ahead. In that way, they made some fast miles, Ben trying to ignore the pain, which was severe. Notsa could see blood seeping its way through the bandage.

"Are they gonna kill us, Father Ben?" the boy called out to him, anxiously.

"Hell no, son. We kill them."

* * *

199

Will saw them coming from his position, where he had an excellent field of fire and they had to ride uphill at him across an open area hundreds of yards wide. He'd set up a solid rest and, waiting until they had entered his kill area, touched off a careful shot. Down there, a man spun from his horse. In rapid succession, he shot four more times, killing another man and crippling a horse, maybe two. The others fled back the way they had come. He waited a few minutes, then pulled out on the trail, following the men cautiously.

* * *

Back on the trail, Drake and Algren held up, then realized that Beck wasn't coming. They had seen Wattley get hit and fall, but hadn't realized that Beck had gotten it, too.

"Jesus, Hoyt, them bastards kin shoot! Thet was six hundred yards or more!" Algren exclaimed. "They musta got Beck, too." He shivered. "An' Pitt and Collins never come back last night. Never heard a thing. Musta got 'em with blades. Never thought I'd see Collins go under from a knife. He was damn good. The hell with it. Think I'll head fer home."

"Guess you're right. Can't take 'em on with just two men. We'll have another chanct at 'em. You go and tell Uncle Port that I need some more men. At least ten. Have 'em meet me at Spencerfield's. I'll foller 'em a ways back."

Algren rode on and Drake got down and built a small fire to make coffee. As the pot started to boil, he thought he heard something. Turning, he looked into the bore of a large caliber rifle, the red eyed man behind it holding it very steady.

"Pour it. Slowly. I could use some."

* * *

200

When Ben held up for the morning coffee stop, they got down and Harp started a fire to make a pot of coffee. A few minutes later, Will rode up with another man, his hands tied to the saddle horn, his bootless feet roped underneath his horse. He glared about him, and Ben saw his mouth was gagged with a kerchief. Will saw where Ben was looking. He smiled.

"Got tired of his bullshit. He told me there's another ten men supposed to be comin' to meet 'em at Spencerfield's. That's that little way-station out of Logan, right?"

Ben nodded. "Ten more, huh? Young must have decided to risk it....or are they working on their own, I wonder?" He got up from his relaxed seat, concealing his pain.

"Notsa, take the kids and start out after Hank. Will, Harp, git 'im down here, close to the fire. I want to ask him a few questions."

Shortly, they had some answers to those questions.

* * *

Drake's body lay in a crevice where no one would find him soon, and the coyotes and other scavengers couldn't reach. The man's deep involvement in the Danites and much of his past activities had come out after Will and Harp had held his hands and feet in the fire a few times. The Aiken killings, the well on Rockwell's land, the various killings of Gentiles and their families. It all came blubbering from the lips of the sobbing fanatic. But it was his involvement with the Perkins train which had doomed him. When Ben heard that, he turned aside and Will, never squeamish, put a bullet through his brain. No way were they going to let a devil like him return to his diabolic activities.

They went on, circumventing Spencerfield's and watching their back-trail carefully. But, evidently the

Danites had given up for the moment. When they got through the pass, they heaved a sigh of relief but their vigilance remained high.

Ben's wounds were healing. "Old *Alstetter's* does it, every time!" He boasted. Added to that, he was a fast healer and Notsa's ministrations were excellent. Though he was in pain yet, in the leg, his arm was doing well and he could use it. When the pain got too great, he resorted to using some of Will's remedy.

* * *

Helena came up, finally, and Ben booked them into the finest hotel, the Last Chance, with special instructions to the livery regarding their horses. Then, at Hank and Will's insistence, he saw a good doctor, who opened one end of the leg injury and drained it, then packed it with sulfa powder and rebandaged it. When he heard about *Alstetter's*, he grimaced resignedly. The arm, he pronounced, was doing fine.

A gold eagle lighter, Ben walked back to the hotel, to find the manager in a tizzy about Notsa and Harp. That handled with an outflow of coin, he rounded up Will and Hank from the bar, found Harp in his room, Notsa and the children in his and took them all down to the restaurant, where, with the gold flowing again, they ate a sumptuous meal, though Harp and Notsa were nervous, in such surroundings and with white people staring.

They stayed there two days, using room service most of the time, to appease Notsa and Harp. Then, Hank took their back-trail and checked it all the way back to the pass. He found it clear of any Mormon party as far as he could tell, and reported back to Ben and the rest.

Ben, meanwhile, had cashed a large check at Wells Fargo Bank and Trust.

"Pay call, boys. You and Will, Hank, are square with me and here's a thousand apiece. Try not to spend it in the first bar you hit. When you git to the end of that, come and see me. Notsa and I are taking the kids down to Harrison and then we're goin' over to my brother's place fer a visit. Harp's comin' with us."

He handed the money over and looking both of them in the eye, he gripped their hands and then gave them a brief hug. They grinned and turned as one, to hit that first bar he'd mentioned. Harp grinned, too. His pockets were full of money.

Brigham Young
by Charles William Carter circa 1870
courtesy of Wikipedia

PART V

CHAPTER 31.

The Last Chance bar was dim with cigar smoke and the reek of beer, whiskey and sweaty bodies: just the kind of atmosphere that Will and Hank loved and right now, craved. Two quick drinks went down with a satisfying loosening of the tension they had been under for days and months. They ordered another and the mustached bartender poured them up with a flourish. They gave him another fat tip and settled back to savor this one. Looking around the establishment, which was nearly full though it was early in the day, Hank could see that most of the men were miners, though there were a sprinkling of other trades evident.

"Ben seemed anxious to be headed back east. S'pose he's wonderin' about Katy. She's the apple of his eye." Hank commented, swirling his glass as he watched the crowd in the reflection of the bar's mirror.

"Yeah, she's always had 'im twined 'round her finger. Wonder if she'll really get to be a doctor. Funny thing fer a woman to want to do, bloody hands all the time, and listenin' to people bitch 'bout their aches and pains."

He took a healthy slug of whiskey and relished the warmth as it went on its way down the hatch. He too, watched the bar mirror. Both men were ever alert around a crowd. Now, he noticed a man who had just entered, an old prospector, from the looks of him. He came up to the

205

bar and put a buckskin poke on it, asking the bartender if he could get a drink from it. The man was apologetic,

"Sorry, old timer, I sent my scales over to the assayer to get reset yesterday and he hasn't brought them back. Here, have one on me."

He poured a stiff drink for the old man, who brought it to his lips and smacked them as he drank it down. "Much obliged!"

Hank watched the old man take the poke and put it in the pocket of a ragged pair of canvas pants held up by a piece of rope. Feeling sorry for him, Hank said, "Wait up, friend. We'll spring for another couple fer ye. We both know what it is to be thirsty!"

The old man looked at them and evidently seemed assured, for he returned to his place and waited while Hank ordered for them. The smell of the old man was rank but both he and Will had suffered much worse.

Two drinks atop the first one loosened the old fellow up and the three were soon easy with each other. He'd been a Union soldier, too, they found, had fought in the ranks of the 2nd Massachusetts through the whole war, was wounded badly at Little Round Top and was delighted when the two told him they had been in Berdan's Sniper Regiment and had participated in many of the same battles.

The day waned as they refought the war, battle by battle, drink by drink. Finally, when the old man seemed about to pass out, they staggered out of the bar together and up the stairs to the restaurant, where they had a big meal. From there, more drinks, then up to their room, where Luke McDougall crashed on their floor, out to the world.

The next day, the old man woke to find his stash still with him and insisted that he go to the bank and turn his gold into cash, asking if they would go with him. They did, and watched as he got $385.00 for his poke. Then, the three decided to go to a haberdashery and buy some new clothes. That done, they retired back to the hotel, where baths were ordered up and a barber summoned.

The trio who came down to the bar was not recognized by the bartender who'd been serving them right along. All of them seemed younger and the old prospector especially, was a different man, freshly shaved and groomed. More drinks followed, with Luke insisting on paying from the proceeds of his poke.

"More where that came from, boys! She's a stunner, a great mine—and no one knows where it's at. Only thing is, I need a stamp mill, 'cuz the gold runs through hard rock and it takes some sledge work to fine it down so I kin wash it."

He called for another and Will asked, "So what's a stamp mill, Luke?"

"Well, it's a machine, ye see, that you runs the ore through and it crushes it down so the fines can be run through a washer that separates the gold out. Comes in various sizes and hammer numbers. A three stamp mill is about right, usually, for a small operation like mine. Pretty easy to transport, set up and can be run with water power, if ye happen to have a stream handy, which I do." He motioned for another drink and the bartender obliged.

"So what's one cost?" Hank queried. They'd been a lot of things since the war but never miners.

"Oh, a new one from Henley's in Frisco runs a thousand 'er so. Then a bunch to get it out here. Happens, though, I know where I kin git one thet's in good shape fer six hundred——maybe less, if I could raise the cash." Another drink went down, then Luke seemed struck with an idea.

"Say, you fellers want ter come in with me? I like ye—we fought on the same side an' all. What do ye say? Got some money? If ye do, an' kin buy the mill, why, I'd go halves with ye. Ye'd not be sorry!"

Will looked at Hank, who shrugged.

"Sure, why not."

Ben watched the Hite wagon train come in from his seat on the porch, where the babies were being played with by Bei under Notsa's watchful eye. Betty had taken to her, after an initial careful inspection that was reciprocated by Notsa, on her part. They had decided to become friends and were soon sharing work and laughter with Felice as Kittledge came through with his usual humor and good will. Ben was happy that they had found some common ground, helped by the children, who needed their care. Bei was fascinated with the babies and was some help with them. Tom was more interested in the new puppies, seven of Brutus's get from a powerful cur bitch that Ben had found in Fort Benton and left with Kittledge.

Ben had detailed the dog to guard the children and that had been his primary job since they had begun their trip home. The night of the attack, he had burrowed down with Notsa and the kids in a shallow hollow that Ben had dug for them, with blankets covering them all. He and Tom had become inseparable and Ben wondered how it was going to work when he had delivered the boy to his grandfolks. Then, an inspiration: he would give him one of the pups. The boy could take it with him and he'd leave Brutus home.

Now, the Hite and Steele wagons were coming over the hill and down into the ford, where the big horses pulled the easy grade up to the barn and into the large meadow where they circled up, still using the defensive mode that had kept them safe many times before.

Ben, watching with approval, saw Freddy loping toward him, the big blazed-faced sorrel swinging easily

208

with a ground-eating stride. He pulled up in front of the house, swung down and came up on the porch to hug Ben. Then he did a double take:

"More kids! Where did they come from?"

His eyes swiveled to Notsa and got wide. Ben turned to her and said, "This is Freddy, my stepson, Notsa. Fred, this is Notsa Begay-Hite. We're hitched, son." For some reason, he was a little nervous.

"The Hell you say! Why, Ben, that's great! Hello, Notsa. Welcome to the family."He embraced her and she smiled over his shoulder at Ben, returning the hug. The kids came up on the porch.

"The boy here was the last survivor of the Perkins train. Tom Tackitt. Meet Fred, my son." Bei climbed up on his lap as he sat down again.

"This here is Bei. She come from down south. We're not sure of how the Navajo got her. Notsa thought it was from the Apaches. Guess we'll keep her." She gave Ben a hug, then climbed back down to go play.

One of the teamsters came up to the porch.

"Hey, Boss? Cookie wants to know where should we put the fire. We still got a quarter of buffalo off that cow you got. Ain't spoiled yet, he doesn't think."

"Put it down there close to the crick where we did last time, tell 'im." The man walked away with a wave at Ben. "H'lo, Hite!"

"Where's Lakey?"

Freddy's face turned grim. "We had a run-in with some French trappers in Benton. The same bunch you had trouble with down at Fort Union. The one you carved up braced me and I had to kill him. Then, later the whole damn bunch jumped Lakey and me and killed him. We ended up hangin' the ones that was left." He shook his head.

"Damn near got me, too."

"Jesus, Freddy, I'm sorry to hear that! He was a good man. I *knew* I should have killed that bastard then, but I got soft, I guess." Ben was upset and remorseful about his friend, a man without enemies.

"Well, anyway, when we opened the safe in his wagon, we found out he'd left his half of the train to me, so I just kept on doin' what we bin doin'. Haulin' freight to hither and yon." He smiled shyly.

"The boys bin callin' me 'Boss.' Startin' to feel like it fits."

"Good fer you, son! You'll do damned well!"

"You taught me, Father Ben. And the work with the guns came in damn handy, let me tell you."

Stamp Mill

CHAPTER 32.

The stamp mill was in Butte and torn down in portable pieces that just fit in a heavy freight wagon, which the owner sold them, too. Draft horses to pull it came dear, and both Will and Hank wished that Ben's horses were available. As it was, a good team cost another four hundred, with harness thrown in.

They outfitted at Sheridan, patronizing Randall's Mercantile there, waited on by the man himself. Ben had told them that if they were ever in the vicinity, they should mention they knew him. They did, and the enthusiastic storekeeper had to be informed of his old friend's whereabouts and how he was doing. That took some time, so they repaired to the saloon, and then it was dark when they got on their way. That suited Luke, who didn't want it generally known where they were going.

They headed southwest, on the road to Nevada City, but turned off before they got there, going up a narrow canyon into the Tobacco Roots Mountains. Finally, they made camp where a small stream was coming down out of a smaller side canyon.

"We got to go up this one here, boys, but we'll hev to do a little work to get the wagon up there." Luke casually mentioned.

The "little work" turned into four days of back-breaking labor, at one point taking a small powder charge, which Luke showed them how to set. At another, the back-breaking toil of unloading and loading the wagon after it had been taken apart and each wheel and the bed hauled over the rocks. Eventually, though, they arrived. At least according to Luke, they were there. Nothing showed: no tunnel mouth, no cabin, no sign of a camp. Just the south face of the canyon.

"Look around. You boys see any mine?" Luke chortled. They confessed they didn't.

Luke hopped over the small stream and pulled away brush to reveal a low opening in the side of the hill.

"There she is, fellahs! Ophir, number 3!"

"Why'd you name it that?" Will said, peering into the dark hole. He shuddered.

"Oh, I always name my mines, "Ophir". After an old girl I used to know, Ophelia, back in Massachusetts." He was unhitching the wagon and hobbling the team. Hank started unloading the camp gear. Will tended to their saddle horses. Luke took them over to a good flat spot and they pitched their tent, started their fire and after a meal of bacon, fried potatoes and flour rolled grouse, complete with coffee laced heavily with whiskey, Luke told them the plan. He pointed upstream,

"We throw a little dam across there, put the spillway right there, then we can position the water wheel, set up the cam gear and then run the belt to the mill, which'll go right about there. Nothin' to it."

'Nothin' to it took another week of more unrelenting labor, something neither Will nor Hank relished, but finally the job was done. In the meantime, the mine had been explored by the men, using carbide lamps which Luke had to show the two how to use. They were complete novices but Luke was patient with them. He, himself was like a beaver, always plugging away, always working cheerfully.

The first trip down into the black opening, where he felt the crushing weight of the tons of earth over his head told Will that he couldn't do it. He just couldn't stand the claustrophobic sensation, the closing in, the pressure. He forced himself, sweating as he did, to follow Hank and Luke to the end of the passage, nearly fifty feet in, where the quartz showed the pick and shovel work Luke had done. That worthy took up the utensil and expertly pried off a hunk of the rock and they carried it out to the light. Will thought the sun never looked so good when they emerged.

They watched as Luke broke up the chunk and showed them the bright yellow band that wove through the rock. The sight of it fascinated them and started them on the way to what Luke and the other miners recognized as "gold fever."

Luke pounded the rock into small pieces, then the pieces into fines that were washed dexterously at the creek in his pan. The glint of the metal shone in the bottom of the receptacle, with one small nugget that Luke carefully picked out with a tweezers and dropped into a tobacco tin. The rest, he adroitly transferred to a soft deerskin poke, smooth side in. Then he smiled triumphantly.

"That's how she's done, boys! That one nugget'll weigh a couple grams. Plenty of pick and shovel work, then wheel barrow it into the hopper, which feeds it into the stamper and out onto the washer." He sat back and said,

"Now, We'll need another set—that's heavy shoring to keep her from cavin' in— and that means takin' the team up and knocking down some more trees, bringin' 'em back here after limbin', and sawin' 'em up so we kin put 'em in place. We kin do thet tomorrow. Then, we'll start in serious-like."

* * *

Two weeks later, the work was divided and going well. Luke mostly did the pick work at the end of the shaft, following the vein. Hank loaded the barrow, shoveling from the muck plate, and wheeled it out to the opening, where Will took over and ran it on to the hopper, where it was dumped. Then, taking the wheel barrow back to the mine, he parked it, Hank having already taken the other back in. Meanwhile, Will was working the stamp mill on the ore, feeding it in and working the washer. When it was full, he yelled and then Luke came out and they took a breather, after which they all grabbed pans and worked the fines. Both Will and Hank had gotten good at panning and the gold was steadily mounting up in the heavy little pokes. Luke was right. The mine was a rich one.

* * *

It was in the fourth week, a fine fall day in late September, after a frost that had started turning the leaves, when during a break, Will said, "Boys, don't look around but I think we got company. Somebody's been watching us from up on the ridge across the crick. I caught a glimpse of 'em the last little while. I think we better ease over to the wagon real casual-like and get ourselves ready fer some visitors."

One by one, they retrieved their weapons, putting on their gun belts and placing their rifles ready to hand.

Another hour, and Will jumped to the mine's opening and gave a piercing whistle. The two scrambled out as four men came riding up, a shepherd dog following them. Will was already behind the wagon with his rifle.

"Watch out, I see a couple up there in the trees with rifles."

Their leader was an older man with long gray hair and a drooping mustache. As he came closer, it was seen that he had a left eye that looked off somewhere else. The one that was focussed on them was as fierce as a hawk.

Those behind him were hard-bitten older men, also. One, on a tall buckskin, was wearing an eye patch. Another was missing an arm, but the hand holding the

214

reins was also gripping a pistol. The last one was riding a splendid black horse and wearing his pistols in two shoulder holsters. He was grinning. The wall-eyed man spoke in a deep, guttural voice,

"Howdy. Been watching you men work like badgers diggin' a hole. Thought we'd help relieve you of the burden of all that gold you bin raking up."

Will said, "Howdy yourself and thanks, but we'll just keep the gold we worked for. And you boys just kick those nags and get the Hell out of here."

"Oh...I think not."

He brought up an arm and the men behind him scattered, all of them reaching for their guns, with two shots coming from above them in the trees. Both missed, but Will's bullet took the leader in the gut and blew him out of the saddle. Luke's hit the two-gun man as he fumbled with his reins and his pistols. Hank's shot got one of the riflemen in the trees. The one on the buckskin wrenched it around and threw a wild shot as he fled. The one-armed man stayed and shot it out, outgunned though he was.

Hank concentrated on the rifleman left, and as he rose to fire again, Hank touched his trigger. The man tumbled down the hill, rolling almost to the creek. Will shot and the one-armed thief screamed and fell, catching his foot in the stirrup. The horse bolted and the man bumped along behind him as his mount followed the buckskin down the canyon. The dog followed behind.

"Both of 'em down up there, Hank?" Will asked calmly, reloading automatically.

"Yep. Hit 'em, anyway."

"Luke, you okay?"

"Sure. Never better. Wish we'd got that last one, though. He might be back with more friends."

Hank got up and, running to the black, who was standing ground tied, stepped into the saddle.

"Hand me my rifle, I'm goin' after that bastard."

Luke threw him his rifle and Hank reined the black around and kicked him into a run.

Will and Luke had pulled the two riflemen down to lay them beside the other dead men, when they heard a rifle shot. Will looked at Luke, who nodded.

They got busy and after going through the pockets and piling money, watches, cartridges and guns, they dragged the bodies to an under-cut ledge upstream on the canyon wall.

"Let's wait a bit. Hank might bring us a couple more." He thought that had been his rifle but wasn't sure.

A while later, as the coffee was boiling and they were ready for a cup, Hank came riding in, with two horses packing limp bodies over their saddles following behind. Again, the dog was trailing behind.

"Had to run the one on the buckskin awhile. Got 'im when he stopped to take a piss. Hated to interrupt him." He dropped the rope and dismounted, came over and took the cup Will offered. Later, they levered the wall of the cutbank over the bodies., covering them with several feet of dirt and rock.

* * *

"Wisht we'd thought to put the tack there before we dropped that bank on 'em." Luke groused as they finished covering the hole that had taken the rest of the outlaw gear, later.

"Yes, that would have been smarter, but we needed to go through it first and those bodies were there in plain sight. They needed coverin'."

Yeah, guess so. Wonder who they were. Never seen 'em before." Luke said.

They had looked through the stuff they'd taken off the dead men and discarded anything that might be traced back to them. Not that they had done anything wrong—- the men were outlaws, pure and simple. But, it was just cleaner to have them disappear without a trace, rather than to have to appear at a Miners trial that might last for days, and also mark them as the ones who done away with them. That might have repercussions, if the men had been part of a larger gang or had relatives who would swear vengeance.

Regretfully, they had stripped the horses and turned them loose, Hank running them down the canyon and out on the valley below that night. The dog followed the buckskin for a ways, then came back and laid down by the caved-in bank. The men were uneasy about the animal. None wanted to shoot it.

"Would have liked to keep that black. That's a dandy horse. But likely stolen." Hank said.

* * *

They had gone back to their mining but the next week, were out of grub, so Will was elected to go to town and resupply. Luke finally voiced what was in their minds,

"Might better take in most of the gold. And boys, before winter hits, we need to throw up a cabin and a stable of some kind. I know there's a man down on the Ruby who would bring us up a couple tons of hay but we need to get a better trail in here. An' next spring, we might think to start haulin' our tailin's. Accordin' to the assay, there's twenty ounces of silver in each ton alyin' there. And we've taken out maybe fifty tons 'er more." He drank hot water as he figured.

Let's see, if silver is three dollars——that makes it worth sixty dollars to the ton. Damn, wish we had a smelter closer than Helena. It's gonna take at least five dollars a 'that to transport it. 'Nother five to smelt it. Maybe forty-fifty bucks to us when it's said an' done. But, still worth it. So I think we need to find some men to come up, do the road work, build the cabin and stable, and maybe some extra sets while they're at it, so we don't have to stop ourselves. And we need to put some meat up. That means huntin' and more time away from working the mine." He sipped his hot water. The coffee was gone.

"Means lettin' people know where our site is. You boys see it the same way I do?" He asked. They did.

"Well, then, let's git the gold ready to go."

Bringing out the little bags and counting them was a work of satisfaction to them, Forty three bags of about six pounds each by Luke's scale at $27 an ounce, which was the rate the last they'd heard, made over $111,000 in the pokes.

"Will, why don't 'cha deposit it in four different accounts fer us there at the Sheridan Bank of Commerce. Thirty-five thousand fer each, then the remainder to the Ophir #3 fer expenses, with each of us able to draw on that one. Sound okay to you men?" It did. THIRTY FIVE THOUSAND DOLLARS!

Suddenly, they were men of substance. Never, in their wildest dreams, had Will or Hank ever thought that they might be rich. But now, with those bags of gold, they were. They grinned at each other.

"Luke, you made it happen. You should rightfully have a larger share." Will said. Hank nodded in agreement. It was the truth.

"Nope. You men've held up your end and came through when it was needed: both when the stamp mill got bought and when those thieves came to rob us. No, boys, she's a straight-away three way split. And more power to us!"

"One thing we need to do, though, is record our claims here. Lige Randall is the head of the Miners Committee, and we kin git 'er done with him. I already set out the claim site and all we got to do is hev 'im set it down on paper and receipt us. Will kin do it fer us, too, when he gits to town."

* * *

Will took the long, hard way back to Sheridan by going on up the canyon until it topped out, then heading east over the ridge until he dropped into the next big coulee and down it until he could top out to the next one, following old elk trails until finally, he came to Wisconsin creek, which Sheridan nestled in. The Fairview and Red Pine mines at the upper end of the creek had necessitated a good road into their operations and when Will hit that, he followed it down until the town came in view.

The bank was open by the time he arrived that morning and before he settled for breakfast, he took care of business there. Off-loading the pack horses and bringing the four heavy mantees in and dumping them on the floor, then opening the packs and bringing out the leather pokes and setting them on the counter was deeply satisfying. The president of the bank, Carson Carruthers, came bustling out when he saw the clerks busy at the task of weighing up the gold, and he saw right away, by the distinctive color, that it came from Luke's mine. But the amount made his shrewd old eyes widen.

He came around the counter and introduced himself. "And who might you be, Sir?"

"Will Kernzy. Luke and Hank Givens' partner. We'll need four accounts." He told him how he wanted it arranged and the procedure was started.

"So what's gold worth right now?"

"Today's market value is $27.80, Mr. Kernzy. Now, Luke may have told you that the bank charges a handling fee of 25 cents an ounce, which we take right off the top. Then also, we charge $10 for setting up each account, also off the top, if that's all right with you." It was. Luke had mentioned the bank's exorbitant rates. He got the deposit slips and the account books for each of the accounts, and with a lightened heart, headed for the restaurant to eat a late breakfast.After that, he went to the mercantile.

219

Randall took care of the recording of the claims for him and instructed his one-eyed clerk to start assembling the supplies on the list.

"Know of any men who might be worth hiring? We need some work done up at the mine."

"Happens I do. The Fairview laid some off and I can steer you right to some good workers, Mr. Kernzy."

The town had seen some downturn in the mining activity lately and now that the Ophir looked to be a going proposition, Randall was eager to oblige.

"If you would like to have a drink over at the Miner's, on me, tell the barkeep, I'll go down to Draper's house and roust him out. And by the way, they been gettin' three dollars a day at the Fairview. Don't know what you intend payin' them, just thought I'd tell you."

They parted at the door and Will went across the street and into the saloon, which was almost empty at that time of day, though men were starting to come in.

Will had his first drink of the day, a stiff one that went down well, then another one. On top of the late breakfast, the two sent the customary warm glow through him. Ever since the Navajo had given him that healing ceremony, it seemed like his leg had given him less pain. Now, even with the long ride, it felt okay, for which he was grateful. The third drink he savored, and as he did, Randall came in with a tall man, his shoulders bent with muscle and work, a long handle bar mustache drooping down almost to his chin. They came to Will and he ordered them one.

"Will Kernzy, Matt Draper. Matt says he kin find you as many men as you need, Will."

They talked awhile and then Will said,

"I need to get back. Round up five of them, then, and saddle 'em up. We'll head out when you get back."

Draper looked blank. "Horses cost money to keep, Mr. Kernzy. We'll be with you on Shank's mare." Will blinked. He would never walk if he could ride.

220

"That reminds me, Lige. We're goin' to need some feed for our hay burners. Kin you contact the farmer Luke mentioned and git some delivered to the mine fer us?" Will asked, glad he had remembered.

"Sure, but the price will be damned high. Likely $30 a ton. Delivered, of course."

Will was partial to the horses, so said, "Tell him we'll pay $35 for his best and better make it six tons."

He turned to Draper. "You'll need to bring some grub. Lige, let them draw on the Ophir. I'll give you a check against it for credit."

He wrote a five hundred dollar check from the expense account and handed it over.

"And Draper, do you know how to set some charges?"

"Sure, any miner worth his salt kin do it. Most aren't as careful as I am, though."

"Well, I'll bring some dynamite along. There's a couple places in the trail that'll need a charge or two."

It was late before they got under way and they camped at the base of the canyon that night. The next morning, after coffee and a decent breakfast of bacon, bread and spuds, they started on their way up what Luke was calling Current Crick.

At the 'Y' they had to thread a narrow, steep walled gorge that Draper soon widened after a stick of dynamite, with the men they'd brought using their picks, sledges and shovels to swiftly clear the trail when the booming echoes had faded away. They went on and a half mile up the rushing creek, came to another wall that had to be widened. That one went down like the first and with the blast, Hank came riding down to see what was going on. They rode together on up and the work party tackled another spot just before the mine: a couple large boulders that needed to be blown and were. Now, a good teamster could traverse the trail up to the mine without any difficulty such as they had encountered with the stamp mill.

CHAPTER 33.

Ben, Harp, Notsa and the kids, with Brutus's pup, Jack, took the *Anson LaFarge* from Fort Benton in September. Harvey Allen met them at the gangplank with the old dog that was his constant companion. "When I heard that you were going to be traveling with us, Ben, I had Stokes reserve the two best cabins. If you don't want the one, just let him know."

Harvey reached out and pumped Ben's hand with vigor, the mutual liking evident. He greeted Harp with a handshake also, uncommon in a boat captain dealing with a former hand. Then he was introduced to Notsa and the children and he in turn introduced them to his old dog. The kids had to show him their new one, and the two dogs touched noses.

"We'll be leaving in an hour. Want to catch this high water and see if we can't ride it all the way to Fort Union. And by the way, I have a new cook aboard. His meal tonight should be grand—-a prime loin of buffalo cow!! You all should enjoy it. See you then."

He left to oversee the last of the loading and the steward escorted them to their cabins and installed their luggage. The boat, Ben noticed, was in good repair: fresh paint adorned the wood work and the decks were swept and clean. the Irish hands, too, seemed cheerful and hard working.

All in all, Ben thought, it was going to be a nice respite from the endless riding. He'd sit with Notsa and the kids on the stern, resting his leg, drinking coffee, and watch the miles go by. He'd decided that the New York trip would be postponed for another time. They'd just go deliver Tom and return home, with a stop-over at Hite Hollow. Linc's work on his folks' farm made him think about their future. He was thinking still he'd like to settle somewhere in the Judith Basin. It was God's country.

* * *

Back at the Ophir, Draper and his fellow workers had just emerged from the mine and were gathered around the fire, having coffee.

"So, you think we should blow through low at the foot wall and take it on down, then?" Luke asked, deferring to Draper, an experienced hardrock miner. Luke himself was more of a glory holer, rocker and pan washer. Surface stuff, mainly. Now, it was a relief to have someone on-site who could give them some expert deep tunnel advice.

"Yeah. A couple sticks should do it. Want me to pound the holes? I threw my drills in the wagon."

"That'd be good, if you would, Matt. What do you think of the lead?" Luke was worried. It seemed to be pinching out, lately, getting narrower. Draper, used to mine owners and their hopes, was evasive.

"Soon as we get this fault blockage out of the way, we'll know more. But it looks good to me. Ore's rich. I see silver in it, and there's platinum, too. After we blow it, I think we better make a couple sets, just to be sure. The rock is strong but I like to be safe."

Will had brought the men and supplies in to a relieved Luke and Hank, who were worried about their friend. Hank was particularly concerned about his pard's tendency to hit the hard stuff, but now was happy that they had sent him. He had come through and done everything they had hoped: deposited the gold, for which they each now had fat accounts, picked up the supplies, hired men and ordered the hay. Now they were listening to some mining expertise which was largely going over their heads but were secure in the knowledge that the men knew their business. Through the trees came a light skiff of falling snow. If they were going to spend the winter, they needed shelter.

They had already paced out the cabin foundation and stable, off to the side at a short distance, and needing some leveling. That work would start tomorrow. The mine's future was what counted right now.

The next day, the work commenced. Draper, Luke and Hank went in and set the charges, while Will and the other men set to the job of erecting the cabin. Will took the team up and they felled trees and brought them down to the site, where a couple of the men who were expert with an axe and broadaxe, got the logs ready to be put in place. Another man searched for, trimmed and set the foundation rocks.

A 'boom! boom!' muffled in the depths of the tunnel and the mouth belched dust and a blast of air.

Hank wanted to go back in right away, but Draper said, "No, we have to wait awhile. Let the air clear some and the fumes go down. Otherwise, you'll end up with a splitting headache and be down for a day 'er two. Bad air'll kill ye."

They went in after an hour and cleared the spoil, then pickaxed the wall some so they could see what the lead was doing. Draper was elated when he saw that the charge had done its work. The lead was right there, bigger than ever. The men were elated. Draper had assumed a leadership role and now stated,

"We need to get after it then, and that means we need rails and a couple good ore cars. 'Course, that means we need to lay ties for the rails. We can cut ties while you take the wagon down and bring us back the rail. One load kin handle that, then another load fer the two cars. Both will fit in a wagon. Don't let them foist off a couple banged up ones with twisted gates on ye. Maybe I should go in with ye. We're goin' to need some more grub. I kin see we got work ahead of us." He turned and shook hands with Luke, Will and Hank.

"Ye got a payin' mine! We just need to get it up and running. And I'd ask Lige to put out the word fer a ten stamper. We kin keep it busy, looks like. We're goin' ta need a mercury plate, too, to collect the gold." He grinned. A paying mine also meant good wages for him and his friends. Suddenly, the winter didn't look so bleak.

* * *

A week later, the cabin was up, and the roof close to being done. Draper was using a wrench on the ten stamp mill that had been set up where the other one had been. He adjusted the cam, which tightened the belt and said, "All right! pull the lever."

One of the men standing by did as he said and the water wheel started turning, then the belt was engaged and the stamps started up and coming down with a crashing, jarring sound. When they were going steadily, Draper motioned to another man and he tipped the ore car, filling the hopper. Ore fed down and into the stamp run and the sound became rock being crushed. Draper nodded to Luke, and the two men watched with a satisfied air as the empty car was pushed back into the mine, the tender pushing it easily.

In a few minutes, another car came out of the mine, and that was dumped. "We're rolling, now. A car every fifteen minutes 'er so. 'Bout right." Draper commented, looking at his watch.

Up the canyon a ways, Hank was saying to Will,

"Well, I'll shoot 'em if you won't. He can't stay there. The men are talkin' about it and we need to do something."

The object of their concern was the dog that had followed the one-armed rider of the buckskin. After they had buried the dead men, the dog had come and taken up a sentinel at the site. He hadn't left, except to go to the creek and get a drink, occasionally. The workers had remarked on it and some had taken food for it. They needed to do something about it but hated to shoot it.

Finally, Will said, "Let me see if I can't get it down to the cabin again. If he won't let me, well..."

He went to the dog and after an initial wariness, it let him pet it. At that, Will slipped a rope over its neck. The animal held back but finally let Will lead it down to the mine, where they tied it and fed it, giving it some bacon scraps and meat from the deer that Hank had brought in the day before. Both were relieved, especially Will. He could kill a man like the master of the dog, who was threatening him, without remorse, but to kill a helpless animal like this dog was something he struggled with.

* * *

Another week and the cabin was finished and the stable, too. The farmer, Ed Quinn, had delivered the hay and a small sturdy corral now held their horses as the snow came down and started piling up.

The dog stayed mostly at the stable, liking the company of the horses more, Will saw. He had become the one the animal took its food from.

The noise of the mill was a tremendous din, and first Will, then Hank, finally admitted that they couldn't handle it. For some reason, Luke and the miners were oblivious to it, concentrating more on what the mill was producing. And that was dazzling! The work had produced another forty bags of the yellow metal and Hank this time,

227

had taken it in to deposit. But to garner this treasure, it was taking back-breaking work down in the mine, and privately both Will and Hank marveled at those men who worked their guts out for three dollars a day and found. Both agreed they wouldn't have done so.

"I'm just not cut out for this mining, Hank! The noise is drivin' me bats for one thing, and you know I just can't go down in that hole. Can't do it! So, I'm thinkin' about selling my share. What about you?"

He was nearly yelling, to make himself heard over the continual ear-splitting roar.

"Hell, I'm with you. I was just waiting 'til you said somethin'. Let's go gather up Luke and Draper and have a confab."

Luke was amazed. Quit? Now? They were making money, well on their way to becoming extremely rich men. How could they turn their back on the goose when she was busy laying golden eggs?

"We're just not miners, Luke! And you are. We know it. Buy us out. What's the mine worth?" Luke looked blank.

"Gosh durn it, I don't know. What do you think, Matt?" He turned to Draper.

"Well, the lead's staying rich as ever and still running about two and three feet wide. We've been catching the gold, but there's silver still, and some platinum, too. I'd think it's worth a lot of money. How much, I couldn't guess. But here, now, if Luke is agreeable, I have a proposition that might be fair to you all. I'll buy in with my experience and take over the shares of you two and give you 40% of my cut of whatever we clear starting tomorrow. What I kin do is just keep putting it in your accounts fer you."

They were all agreeable. They shook hands on it and Luke had a new partner.

* * *

The next day, the two ex-partners loaded their gear into the wagon, tied the two saddle horses on behind, and lifted the dog, which they had named 'Brig' up on the tarped load behind the seat.

"Well, boys, hate to see ya go. Drop me a line sometime." Luke shook hands with them and Draper and the others did likewise. They hupped the team and started down the canyon. It was miles before the sound of the stamp mill faded to nothing. The silence was golden.

* * *

They headed in and stopped at the bank to deposit their share of the last of the gold which had been divided the night before. Added to their accounts, the total was staggering: each had over $100,000. Will turned and asked Carruthers how much he had on hand in cash.

"I want to withdraw a sizable amount, sir."

Hank decided he would do so, too. Each came away with half of their account totals. They threw the burlap sacks of money in the wagon and after stopping at Randall's for some supplies, headed out of town, toward Virginia City. A mile out, they doubled back and took a circuitous route down the valley, bypassing the town to the north.

"Just in case someone might get ideas." Will thought. "Seeing us leave the bank and maybe having a teller—or a bank president for a friend."

* * *

That night, Hank was on guard and dozing when Brig growled. He snapped awake and saw two men skylined, coming toward the camp. His low whistle alerted Will and they were ready when the men shouted "Hands

229

Up!" Both went down with bullets that snuffed out their lives an instant later.

Will said, "I'll take a circle with Brig and see if I can find their horses. They might have left a friend 'er two with 'em."

Will worked his way around a wide circle, coming on two horses tethered in some trees a few hundred yards out.

He watched the place awhile, then quietly went on in and untied them, unbridled them and left them to go back to camp. Hank had already thrown the bodies in the river and made ready to pull out. When Will returned, they got back on the trail, taking it easy and letting the horses pick the way.

They put some ten miles between camps during the night, stopping after they had crossed the Madison and making breakfast. Then they went on to Bozeman. Randall had mentioned there was a gun shop for sale there. That sounded like something they could maybe handle for awhile Worth a try, anyway, and much quieter. And they had worked up quite a thirst, with all that manual labor!

CHAPTER 34.

The *LaFarge* docked at St. Louis in mid-morning. The trip had been a fast one, and for Ben, a refreshing one. They ate well and listened to some good nightly concerts, with Harp and the Irish deckhands blending their voices well on a vast repertoire of songs. Ben could see that Harp had been lonesome for his rivers. When he got to the dock, he asked if he wanted his pay so that he could return to his old job.

Harp thought awhile and then smiled and said,

"Don't believe I do, Boss. Not for a while yet. 'Sides, you might need me on this trip. Ain't over yet! 'Less you wants to cut me loose?"

"I want you fer as long as you want to be with me, Harp! Glad to have you!"

They checked in at the Stockdale and Ben saw that Phikes was still doorman, so made the same arrangement with the Irishman to take care of Harp. Then came a blow-up at the desk, when first the clerk, then the manager, refused to let Notsa stay. It took Phikes, Harp and a policeman finally, to calm Ben down and he told the agitated manager just what he could do with the "whole Goddamn establishment!"

They went, at Phikes' advice, to another hotel, not as ritzy, but very accommodating, especially to anyone who was a friend of Phikes.

Ben was poor company that afternoon but after a delicious meal at the restaurant just across the street, mellowed somewhat and took them all to a variety show. The comedians and the dancing soon overcame the anger and the night ended a success. Notsa and the children were enthralled with the show and asked if they might stay an extra day and see another one. Ben agreed and the next day, after some shopping for them all, which saw them in new clothes and shoes and hats, and Ben buying a watch at Shugart's for Notsa, an exquisite little brooch Bruguet that had quarter and half chimes, they went to another excellent supper and the show. The sides of each ached with the laughter they had done.

The next day, Ben purchased tickets for them on the Missouri and Arkansas Railroad to Springfield, where they detrained for the last leg of the journey to Harrison, the Tackitt's hometown. Ben rented a roomy carriage for the journey.

Tom's reunion with the grandparent there was a stiff, formal one. The elder Tackitt, Abraham, was a lumber mill owner who had been against his son marrying the Johnson girl, against apparently, everything that had to do with how his son lived, from his switching religions to Catholic from the strict Baptist one which so suited the Tackitts, to his deciding to leave for California. At first, he thought Ben was trying to put one over on him, but when he heard the story and saw the boy, who turned out to be the 'spitting image' of his late son, he condescended to shake hands with Tom, who returned the salute gravely. The grandmother, they found, had died the year before. The man left was a miserly shell.

Then, when they were going to leave, Bei, who had been so quiet before, had a fit, not wanting Tom to stay. Notsa had to carry her away, still crying, looking back at Tom who was trying hard not to let go, himself. Ben felt it, too, for the boy had become dear to him. He was a caring, obedient youngster and Ben was going to miss

232

him. Notsa showed that she too, was upset by the parting. Still, the man was the boy's grandfather. Jack, in the boy's arms, looked puzzled at their leave-taking.

* * *

They detoured over to Hite Hollow and Ben was uplifted when he saw what Linc had gotten done in his absence. The house had been added on to, and was re-roofed. There was a new barn with a new corral that had some nice mules in it. The fields were plowed and the kids, who came rushing when they heard it was 'Uncle Ben', were growing and looked sleek and well fed. Linc came grinning from the porch and embraced Ben, shook hands with Harp and welcomed Notsa warmly. The fact that she was Indian was ignored.

Ben had told her about Linc's wife and so she wasn't surprised at Liz's silent greeting. The two had both been through much hardship and it forged some bond that bridged the racial wall and created instant friendship. Ben saw it and so did Linc and Harp.

Monte was there with a handshake, taller, with a muscled grip in his young arm. "I still want to come visit you, Uncle, but Pa needs me here right now. Maybe next year?" Ben agreed, heartily.

The younger children took charge of Bei, who soon was romping with them under the oak tree, being swung in a rope contraption that brought excited squeals from the little girl.

The second day, as they were eating the noon meal out under the spreading oak tree, having a fried chicken picnic with Linc's hired man's family, an exhausted Tom Tackitt, with Jack lolling exhausted in his arms, limped up the lane. He was barefoot, footsore and red-eyed but triumphant.

"Hello! Ben...Harp, everyone. I...just couldn't stay. I want to go home with you!"

He collapsed by the porch, and Ben saw that his feet were bloody. The boy had put some hard miles on, walking barefoot, it looked like, most of the way. He went to him and Tom clasped him around the neck in a rare show of emotion and began to sob.

"Please don't make me go back! I want to stay with you! And Notsa and Harp! That old man don't want me, anyway. Nor Jack either." Ben had difficulty getting his neck from the boy's hard clasp.

"Listen, son, if that's what you want, why, you're welcome to come along with us on home. But why didn't you wear your shoes? They would have saved your poor feet. Look at 'em, Notsa!"

"He took 'em! Said he guessed they might fit him. My hat, too. He was goin' to give Jack away. That's when I snuck out."

He sniffled and Ben handed him his handkerchief.

"Was wishing I had my moccasins, fer sure. But I did catch a couple rides. I ran a lot of the way. I was 'fraid you'd be gone already." He teared up again.

Ben took him over and introduced him to everyone and soon, with Bei coming to hug him, Notsa and Liz doing some doctoring on his feet and Monte bringing him a plate full of food, he was a happy boy.

* * *

There was a half section for sale that adjoined Linc's upper pasture and after he had shown Ben how it fitted in with the farm, Ben went with him to the farmer and they struck a deal for the ground, with Ben giving Linc the money with no strings attached, though Linc insisted he viewed it as a loan, not a gift. Ben didn't care. Linc was a brother and Ben had the money. It was a done deal.

* * *

They journeyed back to St. Louis, their party intact, after all. Tom had known they were going to Hite Hollow but his grandfather had no idea where the boy might have headed for. So now, the Hite family had two children, but Notsa told him there would perhaps be another child in the spring. Ben was ecstatic. It seemed he had known and raised a goodly number of youngsters but so far, none of his own blood. He celebrated by taking them to another show at St. Louis and buying Notsa another piece of jewelry at Shugarts: an emerald bracelet that took her fancy.

It was here that Harp decided to take his leave of Ben. Marsh had seen him on the levy and made him an offer of mate on *Nelly Peck*. It was an offer he couldn't refuse. After Ben paid him, with a hefty bonus, the big man grabbed his hand and nearly crushed it, as he tried to keep the tears from flowing.

"I nebber forgets you, sah! Nebber!"

"Nor I you, Harp. You're a good man. The best! Come up and see us when you can. You can find us in the Territory. Just ask around Fort Benton. Likely, Hite wagons'll be right there on the wharf."

* * *

The St. Louis wharf was lined with boats but Allen's *LaFarge* was off up the Mississippi and Marsh's *Nelly Peck* was not scheduled to leave for another week, so they took passage on the new boat, the Coulson Line's *Dacotah,* which was a huge boat for the upper Missouri and had just loaded 600 tons of cargo. It had two big engines: 18s X 7s, which meant that the <u>inside</u> diameter of the cylinders were eighteen inches and that the piston cylinder was seven feet long. It took at least 30 cords of good hardwood feeding its three boilers to make its daily run.

The captain, Russell Johnson, was an experienced riverman who'd been a pilot and a captain for thirty years. He knew little of Ben Hite, only that the gentleman had purchased tickets for Fort Benton, taking the two best cabins the boat had. He greeted him and his contingent, noting that the woman was an Indian, which meant little to Johnson. He had transported hundreds of that race in his time, though he couldn't remember when one was ever ensconced in his best cabin. 'Would wonders never cease?'

He supposed the squaw man was a rich miner. His watch fob had a large nugget buffalo attached to an expensive Benson and the woman, a handsome looker for a squaw, had a gold Breguet on her luxurious velvet blouse. The kids, though, didn't look half-breed or resemble each other. Or even resemble the father. Odd.

The boat, with much of its heavy cargo destined to be carried all the way to Benton, was shallow drafted but cumbersome, with its length, and frequently gravel or sandbar bound. The captain, though, having had some input on its construction, had made sure the boat had extra stout capstans and tough little donkey engines to run them.

With such a long length and subsequent carrying capacity, it had a surplus of cabins which ran nearly the length of the upper deck. The first of those cabins was by tradition the captain's, situated for his convenience. The next ones were the largest, cleanest and most desirable since they were still in front of the pipes, the big chimneys which continually belched smoke and cinders when the boat was in motion. The others farther to the stern were subjected to the fall of ash and the dense smoke.

It was these first two cabins that Ben had taken, though the purser had said that he'd had an inquiry about them. No money had changed hands for their reservation, though, so he let them go to Ben upon payment.

* * *

236

It was after they had just come aboard, that Ben heard an argument going on right forward of the cabin area in the purser's office. He couldn't make it out but it sounded like objections were being raised about the cabin assignments. He laid on the bed and watched as Notsa put away her and his clothes into the large drawers in the sideboard. A knock on the door brought him up to answer it.

It was the purser, Oakley, and a foreign looking man, a gent with a pencil thin mustache tightly curled above a pursed mouth, tall, silk hat on his groomed head, cane in his hand. Oakley, an elderly man with a frail look about him, was upset and said,

"Sorry to bother you, sir, but would you mind too much if we moved you back four cabins? The children, too? The Count and his party are requesting that I give them the cabins. They insist that they had prior claim, and I do have to admit they did talk to me in that regard. I believe I mentioned it?"

Ben looked at the man with him and took an instant dislike to the shifty eyed creature. He smiled.

"Sorry. The cabins are bought and paid for. I have the receipt right here." He produced it.

"See?" He held it up so the man could read it.

"The cabins are listed by number here and as you can see from the door, here we are."

The purser's face got even longer. The other man's countenance became suffused with anger. He began sputtering in a language which Ben thought might be German. He'd heard it at times during the war. Didn't understand any of it, though. Or give a shit. "Good day to you." He closed the door.

Later, he walked out on the deck to have a smoke and the captain was just coming to see him.

He extended his hand and they shook.

"Captain Johnson, Mr. Hite. I believe there's been a mix-up in your accommodations, sir. My purser tells me that you won't move to some other cabins as he's asked?"

Ben said, lighting his cigar,

"That's right. I asked for the ones we're in. I paid him for them and I have the receipt. Which I showed him. No, we don't plan to move."

"Well, I hate to insist but I must. The Count is an esteemed friend of the owners and the cabins had been promised to him for some time."

Ben smiled. "Sir, you can insist all you or he want. I paid fer 'em and I plan on stayin' where I'm at. My wife likes the view."

The captain bit his lip. He gave Ben a stern look and turned on his heel and strode off.

Ben drew in the first good smoke of the day. He liked a cigar or a pipe, just one or two a day satisfied him. Usually in the evening. And these were good cigars, prime Georgia weed. He'd bought a case of them just before they had come aboard, and from the taste, they were fresh and tasted fine. It was hard to beat Georgia tobacco, though some would debate the subject.

* * *

That night, at the supper table, Ben seated his children and Notsa by him and they were being served when he watched the person who had to be the Count, enter the salon with two other men and a beautiful blonde woman. The steward seated them two tables away from Ben and his party, and as the waiter brought the soup, he noticed that the other table was looking attentively at him. Something was said and the table exploded with laughter.

Bei was still learning table manners and Notsa was not much better at white man's social mores, particularly at the table. Not that Ben was a polished gentleman, himself, or cared to be. He ignored the rest of the people

238

and helped Notsa with Bei and they got through the meal, which was adequate: a pork loin and trimmings, with small carrots and beets.

Afterwards, they repaired to the cabins and Ben got the children settled in and then went to have a drink in the saloon. He entered the crowded establishment and went to the long mahogany bar and ordered a drink. The Count and his men were playing cards at a table and the noise was considerable, some of it generated by those at that table, though much was coming from a dice game in the corner.

Ben watched the Count—Bergdorf, he'd heard the name was, in the mirror. The man had a long horse-like countenance, crossed by a straight scar which went diagonally across one eyebrow and down the length of the face all the way across the thin mouth to the chin. It gave him the look of a man who'd been clawed by a bear, Ben thought. He was young and other than the scar, handsome, and Ben supposed the beautiful woman was likely his wife.

He drank his drink and had another. He didn't care to gamble. His card luck was uniformly poor and he got little pleasure from it, anyway. So after the two, he went back to his cabin.

For being a large, fairly well appointed steamer, it had curiously few avenues of entertainment, other than the saloon and the gambling. There was no band, no piano, no calliope, no chorus, no drama or comedy presentations. Rather, the ship relied on its fairly good kitchen which sold its wares through a small store that charged for each cup of coffee, each doughnut and sandwich. With fuel costing more and more, the purser was determined to see an adequate profit return and as they went up the river, he was satisfied that it was being done, though his passengers were heard to complain. Ben himself was disgusted. His trips with Allen and the other captains had been enjoyable in their free coffee, snacks and lively entertainment.

239

The old purser was also one to hold a grudge. When they met, he made a point of ignoring Ben, as did the captain. The snubs made little impression on him but he made up his mind not to ever ride this boat again.

They had just left Leavenworth, finally, after breaking free from a particularly hard grounding just before rounding the bend that lay below the town, and Ben was ushering his family to the table for their evening meal. The Count and his group came in behind them and looking over the crowded salon, finally took an adjacent table. The blonde woman said something that Ben didn't catch but which he saw that Notsa did. She grew tense and Ben saw that Tom, seated by her, had heard it, too.

"What was that she said, son?"

He looked down at his plate and didn't answer.

"Tom, I asked you what she said."

He looked up. "She said, 'Why do they let Indians eat in here? I might get the plate she ate off the last meal."

Ben scraped his chair back and going to the table, he stood close to the woman, so that she had to look up at him.

"The lady is my wife and is likely cleaner than you are. Certainly, she has better manners. Please keep your crude comments to yourself when you are around me and mine, Miss High and Mighty!"

He turned and went back to the table and wasn't surprised when the man at the Count's right got up and came to the table. He was young and like the Count, had a facial scar. He spoke with a foreign accent and it was hard for Ben to understand him.

"The Count is offended at your boorish remarks to the Countess and asks for satisfaction."

Ben asked, "Is the sonofabitch challenging me?"

The man blinked at Ben's profanity.

"That is correct. Would you name your seconds, please?"

"I have no friends on this boat. You'll have to deal with me."

"Then I would ask what your choice of weapons will be? He smiled, a grimace that looked more like a sneer. "Pitchforks at dawn in some stable, I presume?"

Ben considered, watching Notsa's face. She was as pale as an Indian could likely get. And he could see that she was embarrassed. He silently cursed the narrow attitude that Americans seemed to reserve for other races, even as they espoused the Constitution, which proclaimed that "Men were created equal." He looked up at the young man and said,

"Knives."

The man blinked. "Knives?"

"Knives. Like this one."

He reached back and slipped his ever-present blade from its scabbard at his back. The man stepped back a pace. Then, irresolute, turned and regained his seat. He evidently told the Count what had transpired, for he looked incredulously over at Ben. Ben waved his knife at him, smiling.

242

CHAPTER 35.

The captain knocked on his door that night and Ben invited him in. The man said stiffly, "I would rather speak to you privately, sir."

Ben stepped out and they walked to the rail.

"The word is that you have been challenged by the Count. I just thought that I should tell you a little of his background. He is a noted duelist. He's killed nineteen men in twenty-six duels. Crippled some of the others. His brother, the younger one who looks like him, is just about as bad. They evidently go out quite often in Germany. I wouldn't tangle with him, was I you, Mr. Hite. I might add that this is what I feared might happen and was trying to avoid."

"Well, don't concern yourself. I might ask, though, that if something happens to me, you see my family on up to Fort Benton and my son, Fred Barnes of Hite Freighting, informed."

Johnson was astonished. "You mean...you intend to meet him?"

Ben smiled. "Sure. The sonofabitch needs to be shown how we Yankees do it."

Johnson stepped back. "Well, I have done my duty, sir. I hope you may not regret it. As for your family, I will consider it my duty to care for them."

It was decided through an exchange of polite notes that they would meet at the next stop, which was Yankton, where the boat would spend a couple hours unloading cargo. Notsa was subdued and when Ben told her he'd be fine, she started crying. That made Bei start, and Ben got out of there. He took Tom and they went back to the stern.

"Listen, son. Sometimes you got to stand up for what you believe, your family. Can't let someone show 'em a lack of respect, you know?"

"But what if he kills you? What's goin' to happen to us?" Tom was near tears himself. This man had become like a father to him in the short time they'd been together and now he might die.

"If somethin' does, that's what we call 'Fate.' It's in the cards of life——the way the Almighty has decided it's gonna be. And you'll be provided for. Fred and Betty and Kittledge will take care of you. Just help Notsa and Bei get back to Fort Benton and home. Can you do that for me?"

The boy nodded, too close to tears to answer.

* * *

Yankton

The boat nosed in to the wharf and the deck crew tied up, then rattled down the gangplank. The Count's group was assembled and was first off, and Ben and Tom followed. Notsa was staying on board with Bei but had whispered, as he was going out the door,

"I have prayed to First Woman, to her sons, both great warrior Gods, Monster Slayer and Born of Water, that they help my man when he goes to do battle. They will make your arm strong, your heart big and your strike quick like the sand adder! While you are gone, I will chant the war chant to give you courage."

She turned and gathered little Bei and the puppy to her, then covered them with her favorite blanket. As Ben walked down the plank he could hear her. And behind him he heard Tom whispering the same chant.

They met on the wharf and a crowd had already gathered, mostly from the boat, who had heard of the duel from the steward who had witnessed the altercation. Ben strode into the crowd, which parted, and took off his coat and handed it and his watch to Tom. The Count was already there, a large knife in his hand, his coat likewise off, a smirk of confidence on his face.

The young man, evidently his brother, came forward between them and asked Ben,

"Are you ready to apologize to the Countess? Sir Bergdorf says to tell you that he will consider an apology, if it is properly presented."

"Tell him that the Countess needs to apologize to my wife. Then mebbe I will let him off."

The young man turned and with a stream of German, delivered Ben's answer. The Count's reply was evident. No deal. He turned back and said,

"The Count asks if this is to the death, or just to the first blood. It matters little to him."

Ben smiled. "That's neighborly of him but here in America, it is always to the death. Tell him, by the way, that we are enjoying our rooms and will continue to do so after he's gone."

The Count smiled back. Ben had to give him marks for courage. He seemed without fear. From the boat, he could hear a muffled Notsa, still chanting.

"Then, begin!"

The young man jumped back and out of the way and the Count, using his blade like a sword, came swiftly forward in a classic lunge, which Ben countered with a cutting slash which drew a line of blood from the man's arm. It got his attention and he became more cautious, the arm bleeding. He tried a riposte, which Ben countered with a heavy blow to his face, causing him to stagger back. Then he came swarming forward, slashing with his blade and almost catching Ben as he slipped sideways and adroitly seized the man's extended arm with his left hand. Then Ben drew him in, and as he struggled, and made a deliberate cut across the scarred face, in the opposite direction of the present one, a deep one that immediately began bleeding profusely.

The man let out a bawl of rage and tried to break free but his arm was caught in a vice and his struggle to free it was useless. He threw a blow to Ben's body with his left that Ben shrugged off and the Count's eyes grew wide and fearful as he realized just what he had tackled and that his death was imminent. He caught Ben's arm then, but it made no difference, as his strength wasn't equal to the task of keeping Ben's knife at bay as they strained together. It came relentlessly in, pointed at the man's stomach. Ben's face was inches from the Count's and he grated,

"I kin kill you now, 'er you kin apologize! Your call." The knife touched flesh.

"I...will give my apology!"

Then let go yer knife!"

It dropped from the Count's hand with a clatter on the wharf. Ben backed off, warily. He hadn''t forgotten the brother, whom Johnson had said was as bad as the Count. He was standing there with the servant, his eyes unbelieving. The two men parted, the Count's arm and face dripping blood, his eyes still distended. Ben kicked the knife into the water and stepped up to him.

"I'll expect that apology today 'er I'm comin' after you and this time it'll be your gizzard that my knife tastes!"

He turned and the crowd silently parted, Tom following him back to the gangplank. A smile lighted the boy's face.

* * *

He entered the room and Notsa was still there, still under the blanket. He grinned and lifted it from the two and Notsa's eyes flew open. She jumped to her feet and hugged him, and Bei wrapped about his legs. Jack, catching their emotion, jumped around them and finally into Tom's arms.

* * *

That night, as they sat down at their table, The Count came in, his face heavily bandaged and his arm in a sling, and in full view of the very crowded salon, went straight to Notsa and said, with the young man interpreting stiffly,

"The Count asks your forgiveness for the insult given you by the Countess." Then the Count bowed and took his seat at the next table, facing them.

An interval, and the Countess swept in, and with little accent, addressed Notsa, who had her head down, pointed at the table.

"I, too, owe you an apology. It was...unseemly and unladylike. I hope you will forgive me."

She swept over to her seat with a sullen air,

Ben called the waiter to him and ordered champagne for both tables. The group acknowledged the gesture with bows and the meal proceeded. The salon's noise level gradually regained its normal state.

* * *

Now, the Count courted Ben as though they were equals. He seemed to want to be friends and Ben had no grudge against the man, so they smoked and drank at the saloon together. The Count knew little English so his servant interpreter and the brother were included in their meetings.

"The Count asks that you try one of his cigars."

"Sure, if he would have one of mine." Ben offered. Smoke rose, and over coffee, which the Count had trouble with, due to his badly cut lip, his Highness asked if all Americans fought with the short blade.

"Most do, yes. And also the pistol."

"Is the sword never used?"

Ben blew a cloud of smoke.

"Tell him this is a good cigar. Virginia blend, I believe. Hope he likes mine. No, the reason the sword is seldom used is that, as you kin likely see, very few men pack one. They git in the way out here. But they do carry pistols and knives."

"He says your cigar is good, too. He says that he would like to know more about you. But he understands that it is not, how do you put it, mannerly to ask about one's past on the frontier."

"No, there are men who don't want their past known. I'm not one, though. I have nothin' to hide. Tell him, though, that I would like to know more about him, too, after I answer his question."

The Count was agreeable and Ben told him briefly about himself, including his war years. The men listened with fascination and some understanding dawned as they found out the depth of his experience.

The Count then gave a more detailed account of his background, from his many duels, all with the sword or the pistol, and his experience against the Russians in their later war. The conversation went on for two hours, then the Count asked to be excused, hoping that they might continue the discussion another time. Ben was agreeable.

* * *

They got to be friends, to Ben's surprise. And the cut he'd made across the man's face began to bother him. It nearly matched the other one, leaving the man with an 'X' which stood out and finally he made a weak apology for the ugly gash

"The Count says not to be concerned. In Germany, such scars or wounds are badges of honor and many gentlemen have as bad or worse. He says that he appreciates your thoughtful regard, however."

They drank their coffee and smoked awhile. Then the Count chattered a little in German. The servant, Johann, said, "He wonders if he might ask something personal about your wife?"

"I guess he kin ask. I kin always tell him if it's none of his business." He smiled.

"He just is curious as to what tribe she is. He says she has beauty and a royal bearing about her. Is she a princess?"

Ben chuckled "Wal, she is to me. She's Navajo. From way down close to the Mexican border. You seldom see 'em up here this far north."

"He had seen her with her beautiful blanket. Does she weave them, also?"

"Sure does. I have some in cargo. I'll bring 'em up when we stop at Pierre and show you."

* * *

When Ben displayed the blankets, the Count was entranced and had to have one for his library to display to his friends. Ben said, "Wal, tell him to choose one and it'll be a gift."

He did so, and Ben rolled it up and handed it to him. His Highness was delighted and presently came back with a box of the cigars which Ben had taken a liking to.

A favorite past-time of the passengers was shooting from the stern and one day, as they were sitting there, the Count's younger brother came with pistols and a rifle. Ben watched as they made ready with their weapons and tossing bottles, bombarded them as they bobbed in the wake. Presently, Gregor asked if he wanted to try a shot?

Ben was carrying his pistol as always and pulled it from the holster. "Sure."

He got up, and with his cigar still in his mouth, said, "Throw one." The servant picked one up from the case of empties he'd gotten from the saloon and pitched it high.

Ben shot on the rise as it started to drop and broke it. The Count clapped his approval. "Again!"

Johann threw another and Ben missed, then got it as it hit the water. He laughed. The Count tried his luck and Ben found that he was a fine shot, breaking the bottles regularly, though not in the air. After that, they practiced together often.

* * *

The camaraderie lasted through the voyage until just before Cow Island, when Ben was in his room, chatting with Notsa and a knock came on the door. It was Johann.

"The Count asks if you would care for an evening drink and a smoke on the stern. Both of them are there, already." He seemed ill at ease and left when he had received Ben's assent that he'd be along soon. His gun belt was on the bedstead and he was about to leave without it, when Notsa said,

"Take your gun. I don't trust them. I'm sure it was my prayers to First Woman and the War Gods that made you win against the Count, but I've seen him watching you when he knew you weren't looking and his eyes were not good. Be careful of them, Ben!"

She brought his pistol belt and he threw it on, to humor her, then put his coat over it and checked that his knife was to hand. Warnings like the one that Notsa had just given were to be heeded, he reflected as he went out the door. And maybe her prayers did have something to do with his taking the Count. Whatever. It never hurt to be careful.

The two brothers were sitting by the rail. For once, no one else was about and Ben took the empty chair. Johann brought him a drink, his favorite, a whiskey double with bitters, and lit his cigar for him. He had his hands full and was about to comment on the nice evening, with the stars shining in a glittering cloud of lights about them, when his right arm was gripped by Gregor and the Count came rushing out of his chair with a dagger that took him in the neck, would have slashed his face if he hadn't made a quick move of his head.

The sudden attack was unexpected but Ben had been in too many melees in the war, in which instant action was all that kept him alive. His right arm was immobilized by the brother, who came now with a knife himself and stabbed Ben in the shoulder as Ben rose and with a heave, threw Gregor into the Count, making both men scramble to keep their feet. Ben was hurt but he drew his blade and as Gregor came in, thrust twice, deeply into his middle, quick as a striking snake.

The man bent at the blows and Ben pushed him into the advancing Count again, who had to go around him as he came at Ben. The rushing man was ripe for a counter and Ben dropped to his back as he gripped the man's vest, and threw him over the rail and down into the threshing wheel, which received him and ground him under.

251

The brother was kneeling, fumbling for his dropped knife and Ben, in a rage now, grabbed him at the shoulders and picking him up, heaved him over the rail also, into the turning wheel.

He was hurt——maybe unto death, but after groping with his left hand, could tell that the wound to his arm was minor compared to the neck thrust, which was deep and bleeding bad. He felt about to pass out and Johann came as he stood there swaying and said, as Ben held his knife on him,

"Let me help. I didn't want to mix in it but I should have warned you. They'd planned it ever since the duel. I'm not armed."

Ben looked at him and said, "Get me to my cabin and we'll call it square."

Notsa didn't scream when the two came in, Ben dripping blood all the way from the stern up the gangway to the cabin door. She got him onto the bed and together, she and Johann got his shirt off and tried to staunch the flows from the two deep wounds.

Tom heard the commotion and came to the door and Johann said,

"Quick, run to Doctor Beadle and have him come. Hurry!"

Tom took off and shortly brought back the portly doctor, who took charge. He'd been in the war and knife injuries were routine to him. Presently, with Ben barely conscious from the blood loss, he went to the wash basin and called to Tom, standing by, for more water. The boy rushed out.

"He's lost a lot of blood. The one on his neck nicked an artery, fer sure. Went into the lung, from the looks of it. But I got it stopped and sewn, and the other taken care of, and I <u>think</u>, he'll live. What the <u>hell's</u> goin' on?" Johann answered him,

"The Count and his brother were determined to kill him. They waited until no one was present and attacked

252

him on the stern. They were going to throw him over after they'd killed him. But, he threw them over, instead."

"You're their servant, that right?" Doc Beadle asked, his old eyes steady as he toweled his hands off.

"Yes, I was but that doesn't mean I'm a murderer. I didn't have a part in it. You can ask Hite. He'll vouch for me."

"What about the Countess? She involved?"

"She knew what they were going to do but advised against it. I don't know what she'll say."

"Well, the captain'll have to sort it out. It's his responsibility. I'm going to see him now and then come back. In the meantime, keep him quiet and very still, you hear?" This he addressed to Notsa, who nodded. Her fears had been correct, after all. She knew it!

* * *

The ship was in an uproar the next day, with Johann having to tell his story a half dozen times, as the captain, hearing the two men were overboard, turned around and ran back to where they thought the bodies might be. One was found at mid-day, lodged against the bank. It was Gregor and he was beaten badly by the wheel's paddles, but recognizable. A full day's search never came up with the Count, however, and over the Countess's objections, the boat headed back upstream.

* * *

Ben was holding his own. He had come to, and the doctor, knowing his patient, had prescribed liquids and soup to replace the blood as much as possible. The captain had just left after getting his statement, the purser writing it in a cramped hand. Now, Notsa was getting ready to feed him.

253

"You tried to tell me, Luv, but I didn't listen. If Johann had sided with 'em, too, I'd be dead right now." He said weakly as she spooned chicken broth into him.

"It was First Woman who saved you. She and Monster Slayer, for that is what those two were— monsters!"

"Honey, I bin thinkin."

She interrupted him with a spoonful of soup.

"There's a hot spring a couple miles from Betty and Kitt's—it's over northwest a little ways in the foothills and on the creek—-that would make a nice place to settle down. We kin buy a stud and some real good mares and raise us some horses." He patted her stomach. "And maybe some kids, too."

She smiled. Her man was going to get well. He was a warrior! If only she could have a Blessing Way ceremony for him. —-But maybe her prayers would be enough. They certainly had been powerful, so far!'

"And Luv, remind me to tell Doc about *Alstetter's Remedy*. I wonder if the boat has any?"

ABOUT THE AUTHOR

Dave Lloyd is a 4th generation Montanan whose great-grandmother came up the Yellowstone on a steamboat to the head-of-track outside Miles City. She knew and told her family stories of the men and the women who lived at the time. Dave grew up listening to her and his grandmother, the first white baby born in the county, as they reminisced of that era's rowdy times.

As a young man, Dave was a working cowboy and became assistant ranch-manager on one of the largest ranches in the state, Western Cattle Company, with hundreds of sections of land and cattle numbering in the thousands. The harsh Montana winters gave Lloyd the incentive to leave the rigorous ranching life and get a higher education.

After attending college and becoming an educator, then school superintendent, Lloyd began to write of the early beginnings of the state he loves. He researches his books and tries to make them historically accurate, with their characters true to the times.

Now retired, Dave Lloyd and his wife, Donna, divide their time between Lake Havasu City, Arizona and Helena, Montana, where Lloyd continues to research and craft his novels.

THE STORY CONTINUES

Read book three of the Ben Hite trilogy, LEGACY.

Made in the
USA
Monee, IL